Praise for
Marguerite Duras

"Marguerite Duras leads us into her characters with such grace and power that we don't know what she's done until they take us over."
—Judith Rossner

"A spectacular success. . . . Duras is at the height of her powers."
—Edmund White

"The sentences lodge themselves slowly in the reader's mind until they detonate with all the force of fused feeling and thought—the force of a metaphysical contemplation of the paradoxes of the human heart."
—*New York Times*

"Duras stands perennial and relevant, effecting and fraught. Any chance to encounter her psychological terrain is cause to awe, to be shaken out of compliant identification, comfortable desire, and to slip the frame."
—Douglas A. Martin

"Duras's writing has real power. Her strength is in her images, in the music of her prose."
—*New Republic*

"Duras's language and writing shine like crystals."
—*New Yorker*

"Duras writes exquisitely . . . with a brilliant intensity that is rare outside of poetry."
—*Daily Telegraph*

Select Books by Marguerite Duras in English Translation

Sabana

Abahn

David

Translated from the
French by Kazim Ali

a novel by
Marguerite Duras

OPEN LETTER
LITERARY TRANSLATIONS FROM THE UNIVERSITY OF ROCHESTER

First edition, 2016

Library of Congress Cataloging-in-Publication Data: Available.
ISBN-13: 978-1-940953-36-6 | ISBN-10: 1-940953-36-7

Printed on acid-free paper in the United States of America.

Text set in Garamond, a group of old-style serif typefaces
named after the punch-cutter Claude Garamont.

Design by N. J. Furl

Open Letter is the University of Rochester's nonprofit, literary translation press:
Lattimore Hall 411, Box 270082, Rochester, NY 14627

www.openletterbooks.org

to Robert Antelme
to Maurice Blanchot

Abahn
Sabana
David

Night comes. And the cold.

They are on the road, white with frost, a woman and a young man. Standing stock still, watching the house.

The house is bare inside and out. The interior still unlit. Beyond the windows a tall man, gray-haired and thin, looks in the direction of the road.

Night deepens. And the cold.

There they are, in front of the house.

They look around. The road is empty, the sky dark against it. They do not seem to be waiting for anything.

The woman heads up to the door of the house first. The young man follows her.

It's she who enters the house first. The young man follows.

She's the one who closes the door behind them.

At the far end of the room: a tall thin man with gray hair watches them enter.

It's the woman who speaks.

"Is this the house of Abahn?"

He doesn't answer.

"Is it?"

She waits. He does not answer.

She is small and slim, wearing a long black dress. Her companion is of medium build, wearing a coat lined with white fur.

"I'm Sabana," she says. "This is David. We're from here, from Staadt."

The man walks slowly toward them. He smiles.

"Take off your coats," he says. "Please sit."

They do not answer. They remain near the door.

They do not look at him.

The man approaches.

"We know each other," he says.

They do not answer, do not move.

The man is close enough now to see them clearly. He notices that they will not meet his eye.

She speaks again. "We're looking for Abahn. This is David. We're from Staadt."

She fixes her large eyes on the man. David's gaze, behind his heavy lids, is inscrutable.

"I am Abahn."

She does not move. She asks:

"The one they call the Jew?"

"Yes."

"The one who came to Staadt six months ago?"

"Yes."

"Alone."

"Yes. You're not mistaken."

She looks around. There are three rooms.

The walls are bare. The house is as bare inside as it is outside. One side abuts the road, white with frost, the other borders the depths of a darkened park.

Her gaze returns to the Jew.

"This is the house of the Jew?"

"Yes."

In the park, dogs bark and howl.

David turns his head, looks toward the park.

The howling dies down.

It's quiet again. David turns away from the park, back to the others.

"You were sent by Gringo?"

She answers:

"Yes. He said that he would come later."

They are silent then, the three of them standing there. The Jew approaches David.

"Do you recognize me?"

David looks down at the floor. She answers:

"He recognizes you."

"You're David, the stonemason."

She replies, "Yes, that's him."

"I recognize him," says the Jew.

David's eyes are fixed on the floor.

"He's gone blind," says the Jew.

They do not answer.

"He's become deaf."

They do not answer.

The Jew approaches David.

"What are you afraid of?"

David looks up at the Jew and then back at the floor.

"What are you afraid of, David?" the Jew asks again.

The gentleness of his voice elicits a shudder from behind those heavy-lidded eyes. She answers:

"Nothing. He's a member of Gringo's Party."

The Jew is silent. She asks:

"Do you know what that means?"

"Not for David," says the Jew.

For the first time, Sabana looks right at him. He is looking at David.

"But for everyone else, you do?"

"Yes."

A sudden exhaustion sweeps over the Jew.

"You were waiting for us?"

"Yes."

He takes a step toward David. David doesn't flinch. He comes closer. He lifts a hand. Gently touches David's half-lidded eyes. He says:

"You've become blind."

David jumps back. He cries out:

"Don't touch me!"

David raises his hands, made swollen and cracked by working with stone, and says:

"Don't do that again!"

She looks from one to the other without moving. She says nothing.

The Jew backs away. He returns to the chair he was occupying when they first came into the house, the one near the table.

"You're not scared," he says, "You have nothing at stake. Take off your coats. Sit. You're not going anywhere."

They remain as they are, erect, alert, near the door.

Calmly, she speaks.

"You don't understand. We've come to watch you."

"Watch me."

"Don't try to run away."

"I won't."

"It's not worth the trouble."

David is silent. Sabana points out the Jew to David. She repeats what she said to the Jew.

"He knows it's futile to try."

"I do know," says the Jew.

It's Sabana who takes off her coat first. She puts it down near the door. She helps David with his coat.

Tucked into David's belt is a gun.

They sit. Sabana pushes an armchair toward David. She sits in another chair.

The Jew is silent.

She sits up straight, looks around. She looks out at the road, the park, the cold. Everything is bathed in the same intense light, inside, outside. Nothing else is lit up. She looks over at the one sitting next to the table.

"We wait for daybreak," he says.

Sabana's eyes are blue—dark and blue.

"You're Sabana."

"Yes."

The dogs howl in the dark park.

David listens to the dogs.

The howling dies down.

Silence.

David the mason reclines his head on the back of the chair, his hands draped along the armrests. He looks over at the far end of the room. He speaks.

"There's someone else in the house."

"It's just me," says the Jew.

"He's here alone," she says.

"The Jew," says David.

"Yes. Don't be afraid."

She is still looking around. She is perched on the edge of her seat, still alert. Looking around.

"David has to work tomorrow morning. He has to sleep a little. If you try to run I'll yell and he'll wake up."

"Let him sleep. You keep watch on me. And I'll stay where I am, over here."

Slumber settles on David. He looks over at the Jew.

She says:

"He's falling asleep now."

The Jew does not answer. Sabina speaks:

"The merchants' police aren't out tonight. Gringo made a deal with the merchants. They told him, 'If you let us sell to the Greeks then we'll give you Abahn the Jew.' Gringo agreed. The police sleep tonight. The town is Gringo's."

The Jew does not answer, does not move.

"Are you going to try to run away?"

"No."

The Jew's exhaustion seems to grow.

"Why not?"

"I have no desire to save myself."

They sit quietly for a moment. Sabana, alert, turns toward the frost-covered road.

David has closed his eyes.

"Why did you come to Staadt?"

The Jew shrugs his shoulders.

"To kill Gringo?"

"No."

"Gringo is strong in Staadt. He runs the show with the merchants. He runs the government offices. He has his own police, army, guns. He's been making the merchants afraid for a long time now. You understand?"

"The merchants of Staadt aren't afraid of Gringo," says the Jew.

"Since when?"

"For a long time. The merchants are afraid of the Jews."

"And who is Gringo afraid of?"

"Gringo is afraid of the Jews."

"Like the merchants?"

"You know that."

"Yes," Sabana looks at him.

"You don't know what to do with yourself anymore, do you? So you came here?"

"Maybe at first. But then I found Staadt."

"Like any other place?"

"No."

They fall silent. David sleeps.

Sabana points at him, says to the Jew, "They all sleep."

They look at each other. Still silent. She waits. He asks:

"Who are you?"

She hesitates. She looks at David.

"There's nothing here," he says. "I am not part of Gringo's party."

She is perched on the edge of the chair, waiting. She asks:

"Are you an enemy?"

"Yes."

"What did you want?"

"I don't know what I wanted anymore."

They look at each other in silence for a drawn-out moment.

"Who are you?" he asks again.

He waits. Her eyes narrow, searching. Her face is unreadable. She opens her eyes and says:

"I don't know."

The Jew slumps forward over the table. He rests his head in his arms. He stays like that without moving. She asks:

"You didn't want anything?"

"I didn't want anything. I wanted everything."

Silence.

"And tonight?"

"Everything. Nothing."

"Still?"

"Yes."

His face can no longer be seen.

"One day you came to David's workshop. You waited until the workday was finished. It was David who saw you. He asked you, 'Are you Abahn?' You said yes. He asked you, 'What do you want?' You said 'I wanted to talk to someone.' He said, 'Who?' You didn't answer. You just looked at him. He said, 'Are you looking for David? That's me.' You said yes. He asked, 'Why?' You said, 'Because you addressed me.'"

The Jew is silent.

"You remember."

"Yes."

"That's when all this started."

He doesn't say a word, doesn't move.

"I'm telling you, I'm explaining it to you, aren't you listening?"

He isn't listening.

Sabana, at full attention, watches him.

.

T he night deepens. And the cold.

Someone has come in, a tall man, thin, graying at the temples.

Sabana watches him enter. The man smiles at Sabana. She does not smile back. He says:

"I was passing by."

They look at each other. He looks away, sits down next to David, away from the Jew.

"Close the door. It's dark, it's cold out."

He goes to close the door, comes nearer to her. He gestures toward the frost-covered road beyond the uncurtained windows. Then toward the Jew.

"I was passing by. I saw someone crying. I came."

The deep blue gaze of Sabana now fixed on the newcomer.

"Who are you?"

"They call me Abahn."

"His name is also Abahn, but we call him the Jew. Gringo had a meeting this evening. We're guarding this one until he comes. He said he'll come at daybreak."

"Before the light?"

Sabana doesn't respond immediately. Then:

"Yes."

Abahn has noticed that David is asleep.

"That's David," Sabana says, "the stonemason. I'm Sabana. We're from the village of Staadt. From Gringo's party."

She turns then, gestures toward the Jew, resting his head on the table.

"I don't think he's crying."

Abahn looks at the Jew.

"He is crying."

She looks then at the one who is crying. Then the one who is speaking.

"He can't be crying, he wants to live."

"He's not crying for himself," says Abahn. "It's an empathy for others that forces him to cry. It's too much for him to bear alone. He has more than enough desire for himself to live, it's for others that he can't live."

She looks at him with interest, his white hands, his smile.

"Who are you to know all this?"

"A Jew."

She studies his smiling face, his hands, his manner, for a long time.

"You're not from around here."

"No."

She turns away from the night and the cold. "We call him Abahn the Jew, Abahn the Dog."

"The Jew, also? And the Dog?"

"Yes."

"And the other Jews here? You call them that, too?"

"Yes."

"And the dogs?"

"We call them Jews. And where you come from?"

"There as well."

Her gaze returns to Abahn.

"Are you an enemy?"

"Yes."

"Of Gringo only?"

"No."

She does not move at all for a moment, her eyes open, vacant. Then she waves a hand once more at the one who is crying.

"We don't know anymore whether he is himself. An enemy, too. He's not from this place after all.

"We don't know where he comes from.

"He'll be dead at daybreak."

Silence. She continues:

"They don't kill them every single time."

In the shadows her blue eyes train themselves on Abahn.

"There are no gas chambers here."

He answers slowly, his gaze frozen.

"There aren't. There never have been."

"No."

"There aren't any anywhere anymore."

"No, there aren't any anymore."

"Nowhere," says Abahn.

Sabana's gaze empties out once more. He says:

"Nowhere." He looks at her, says again, "Nowhere."

"No."

She is quiet again. Then she gestures in the direction of the road, at something no one else can see. Her voice is flat, her stare vacant.

"The ones they leave alive are sent to the salt mines in the North," she pauses.

"The ones they kill they bury at the edge of the field—" she gestures off. "That way."

"Under the barbed wire."

"Yes. No one knows that."

He does not answer.

"It's barren, no farming there. The merchants and tradesmen gave it to Gringo after the war for his parties."

He has not taken his eyes off of her. He asks:

"There aren't any more parties?"

"The last ones were deserted. It's been a long time since then."

"The young people don't come anymore?"

She doesn't know, it appears. She is distracted.

"I think so, I don't really know."

Her stare is always empty, her voice always flat.

"You could kill them one by one," she says slowly, "in the Nazi gas chambers."

"Yes. But not anymore. There aren't any chambers anymore. Anywhere."

"No. No, here you get the labor camp or a quick death."

"Yes."

Her blue eyes slash always in the direction of the road. She says:

"It wasn't these Jews here in those gas chambers."

"No, it was others."

"Others," she pauses, "but the same name: Jews."

"Yes. We wanted that."

She asks nothing more.

He looks at the bare walls, the white road white with frost, the darkened park beyond.

"It was his house," he says.

"Yes. And there's a park. There. And in the park there are dogs."

Her gaze comes back to the space in front of them.

She gestures toward the back of the house that opens onto the park. "There's this room that looks out on the park, the other you came from. If you try to run away, I'll call out to David. David will wake up and he'll kill you."

He smiles. She says:

"That's the way, here in Gringo's houses in Staadt. They shoot, they kill. Unless we tell them that they don't have the right, then they don't have the right. Before it would take a little longer."

"And whose territory are we in now?"

"The one who is the strongest. During the night that would be Gringo."

"And in the day it's the merchants."

"Yes," she says. "Before, a long time before Gringo."

Abahn gets up, he walks back and forth across the room, going and coming, and then he sits near the Jew, on the opposite side of the table from him. She joins them. She sits with them. They look at the Jew. She talks, is quiet some more, talks again.

"He didn't know where to go when he came here. He came here because he didn't have anywhere else to go. He's been here for a few days already, waiting for us. The merchants were also looking to get rid of him, as you see."

"Yes."

She looks at Abahn for a long time.

"And you?"

"I came to Staadt now, tonight."

"By chance?"

"No."

Silence. She is still focused on him.

"You're alone as well?"

"Yes. With the Jews."

He smiles. She does not return his smile. It is almost as if she doesn't see it. She says:

"This house is being confiscated by the merchants, the park, too. Not because of the dogs; we don't know what will happen to them. They find it hard to adjust to a new master. We don't know what to do with them."

"Maybe. Did the Jew have anything to say about it?"

"Not yet."

He looks at her more intensely.

"Did you ask him that question?"

"Which one?"

"About what is going to happen to the dogs?"

She turns toward the dark park.

"Maybe later," she says, "later in the night."

David shifts in his chair. He opens his eyes.

Then falls asleep again. Abahn says:

"David wakes up when we talk about the dogs?"

"Yes. You guessed it."

The same slowness creeps into their voices. He asks:

"Why did you let me in? For what?"

She says quickly:

"You came in."

"Why did you speak to me?"

"You spoke to me."

Abruptly his glare flares, then subsides.

"You're not afraid of anything," he says. "Nothing."

Silence. He regards her slim form, erect, alert. Her half-lidded stare. She listens out the window: the dogs are barking.

Far, in the direction she listens, that of the setting sun, the dogs are barking. Muted but numerous.

The barking ceases. He asks:

"Are you afraid now?"

"Not as much."

"You're not afraid for yourself?"

"No." She pauses, considers. "Not fear."

He waits. She is thinking. She finds what she wants to say:
"It's to be suffered."
"Badly?"
She considers again:
"No. In full."
They fall silent.

·

Shegets up. She walks toward David. She gestures toward Abahn. She speaks in a low tone. "They know each other a little, David and the Jew."

She is listening to the sounds of Staadt outside.

"I think they are still coming."

She turns in the direction of the frost-covered road, pauses.

"You said they knew David a little?"

"Yes. Some people knew him. David may have forgotten, but they knew him." She pauses again. He says nothing. She turns to him.

"What did you say?"

"Nothing."

They look at one another.

He asks:

"Who are you?"

She focuses on him, his intense gaze, interrogating.

"I don't know," she says.

His stare bores into her.

"I mean to him—who are you to him?"

She shrugs. She does not know anymore.

"Are you his wife?"

"Yes."

"Are you his mother?"

She does not answer. She is thinking.

"You're not his mother?"

"He wishes I were his mother."

"You don't want that?"

"No."

The Jew raises his head. She sees him. For a long while she looks at him. Then she goes to sit down next to him again. She is quiet the whole time. Then she speaks to him in even tones:

"You wrote. You talked with people. You didn't work."

She is talking to Abahn.

"He walked in the streets, the avenues, night and day. He went to see the shipyards. From time to time he went to the cafes to talk with people."

"He spoke to them?"

"Yes, he asked them many questions."

"And David too?"

"Yes, David too. From time to time you would tell them some things difficult to follow, as if they could understand. And then it was explained to us what you were saying."

"Gringo?" asked Abahn.

"Yes."

She is trying to remember.

"He said, 'Liberty.'"

"And how did Gringo explain it?"

"Money."

"He said, 'Underneath the truth.'"

"And how did Gringo explain that?"

"Crime."

"He said, 'Live into the future.'"

"And how did Gringo explain that?"

"Proof."

She thinks. She asks the Jew:

"What did you say?"

"Don't believe anything anymore," says the Jew.

"Nothing. No one," says Abahn.

"Not even you?" asks Sabana.

"Not me, not him, no one."

"Not him?"

"Not him. How would Gringo put it?"

"Don't listen to Gringo anymore."

They fall silent. Sabana considers what the Jew said.

"He said, 'You should be happy no matter what.'"

"How would Gringo put it?"

"He didn't explain."

Sabana, her eyes on the ground, in a dream, for a long moment. Then she speaks without shifting her gaze.

"Where would he go if they let him go?"

No one answers her.

"And if someone grabbed David's gun?" she says. "I've never left Staadt. I don't know anything about what's beyond."

"Are you thinking about the Jew?" asks Abahn.

"I'm thinking. Where would he go?"

"Beyond here," says Abahn, "more Staadt, other Jews. And beyond that more, an unending chain all the way to the border."

"Until when?"

"The sea. And then along the bottom of the sea."

She is dreaming.

"It's fully occupied?"

"Fully."

Silence.

She looks away at the invisible distant border. The Jew, unmoving, watches.

"Other Jews," she says.

"Yes, and other Gringos," says the Jew.

"Merchants or no," says Abahn, "other Jews, other Gringos, all the same."

She is still looking off into the distance.

"It wouldn't do any good to run away then," she says.

"No," says the Jew.

Again sounds the muted barking of the dogs, their growls rising, in the direction Sabana looks.

She says:

"Those are the dogs of the killing fields."

Silence.

Abahn asks:

"Are there many dead?"

Sabana seems uncertain.

"They say twenty million in all. I don't know about the dead."

Sabana's gaze returns to them. The Jew still watches.

•

The cold deepens still. And the night. The sky is nearly gone. The park completely in shadow.

"It's the ice," says Sabana. "Outside you walk on the road—you slip, it'll kill you."

"We are locked in then," says Abahn.

"Together," says the Jew.

Silence.

The dogs howl, those belonging to the Jew, close by, in the park.

Like every other time, David briefly rouses.

Abahn stands, slowly turns around the room, then walks toward David, stops in front of him. Sabana watches him.

"How old is he?" asks Abahn.

"Twenty-five," says Sabana. "Married to Jeanne."

"Neither Jew nor dog, ever?"

"No."

He gestures at David's calloused hands. "A laborer?"

"He's not qualified for it, he works on the Portuguese crew."

He comes closer to David. Sabana does not move.

"And whose gun is it?"

"It's Gringo's."

"Taken just for tonight?"

"Yes."

"To execute the Jew?"

Sabana turns toward the Jew. He does not look like he is listening.

"No. Just to keep him here."

"So it's Gringo who's in charge of the Jew's execution?"

"Yes. Gringo."

"You're sure? Gringo?"

Her eyes widen suddenly with fear. She gestures toward David.

"Look, do you think he's too young?"

"No. He's already got a gun on him, hasn't he?" says Abahn.

She turns back to the Jew. Eyes still wide.

"You said something?"

"No."

Silence.

"Who will kill you?"

The Jew doesn't answer.

"David?" asks Abahn.

She doesn't think, just answers:

"Why would David kill the Jew?"

The Jew's voice comes so softly, one could hardly understand what he said.

She is not looking at him anymore. She repeats:

"Why?"

They do not answer her. She answers herself.

"So that Gringo won't?"

They still do not answer. She says:

"If it was David who killed the Jew, then who would you say killed the Jew?"

"David," says the Jew.

She looks at Abahn.

"You heard what he said?"

"Yes."

"Well, answer him."

"I say if Gringo kills the Jew, only then would it be Gringo who would have killed the Jew."

"I say no. I say if it's David who pulls the trigger, it's still Gringo who has killed him."

"No," says the Jew.

She stands and up and stares them down. Her glare is cutting. She addresses the Jew. "Explain."

"We can talk about what Gringo said later," says the Jew in a low voice.

"Later after what?"

"After David has shot the Jew."

She is silent.

She looks at them, one after another. She pauses, they say nothing. She cries out:

"I want to understand."

"Do it," says the Jew. "Understand."

She sits there, facing him, completely still.

That violent blue stare.

"The merchant's police have abandoned the Jew to Gringo so he can kill him," she says, her voice faltering.

"Probably," says Abahn.

"They are agreed on this. Gringo said to them, 'Don't get involved in this, the thing I ask of you.' 'Understood,' said the merchants. And there you go, Gringo and his Jew to kill."

"Yes."

The Jew smiles. She does not see. She speaks quickly, "And there is Gringo with his Jew in his grip. And there are the police of merchants just waiting for Gringo to have killed his Jew."

"No," says the Jew.

"And there are the tradesmen's police who are waiting to be able to say: 'Here is Gringo, the one who killed the Jew.'"

"Yes," says the Jew. "Like that."

"And then Gringo who will be able to say: No, the one who

killed the Jew is the one named David, a mason from Staadt. You're mistaken, you've been fooled, it wasn't me, it was David, a mason from Staadt."

"Like that," says Abahn.

"An unlucky Gringo?"

"No."

"An acquaintance of the Jews?"

"Yes."

Silence.

She walks away. Toward the window. Then a moan of anger, of sadness. She looks through the window at the night, lingering. Then roughly she turns toward the Jews.

"And if it isn't David?"

They do not answer.

"Who would it be?"

Her question asked, she doesn't wait for the answer. She answers herself, staring at them:

"It would be nobody, maybe?"

She turns toward him, the Jew, she sits there, before him, in front of him. There's a moment of clarity—the setting sun pierces the place and illuminates it with yellow light.

"Who are you to create such fear?"

The sun sets.

"Who knows?" says Abahn. "Suddenly out of the blue, one Jew too many?"

"Killed?"

"Yes."

"The one who upset the merchants?"

"No, because the merchants agreed."

"Who?"

"The one who agitated the other Jews," says Abahn.

She wants no more to account for death.

"We speak without understanding," she says. "It's so difficult to understand."

"Yes," says the Jew.

Abahn walks over to stand next to her. She notices him suddenly.

"Why did you come?"

"I saw someone crying."

"A Jew."

"Yes. I know them."

"Racists are executed here."

The blue eyes darken.

"I'm a racist," says Abahn.

They do not take their eyes from one another.

"You're Abahn the Jew, Abahn the dog?"

"Yes, that's me as well. Didn't you recognize me?"

"Yes." She looks from one to the other. "You're the one who will not be killed."

"Perhaps."

"The one who speaks?"

"I speak for the Jew."

"The one who sees? The one who will speak?"

"Yes."

"To whom?"

"To those who see and understand."

Sabana turns toward David, his eyes closed. She gestures. "And to him as well? The deaf and dumb? And to apes?"

"Them too, yes," says the Jew.

"Ha!" An explosion of silent laughter mars Sabana's face.

"We will seek their ears," says Abahn.

"Their eyes," says the Jew.

"To understand them," says Abahn.

"Their conversation," says the Jew.

Silence.

She looks at them, first one, then the other, then at David. "And the others who are yet to arrive, perhaps?"

"Perhaps," says the Jew.

"The night is long," says Abahn. "Long and empty."

She turns in the direction of the road. "And where did you both come from?"

"From everywhere," says the Jew.

She takes one step toward the door that leads out to the park. She stops. A last light slides down the walls and goes out.

"They kill them quickly, usually," she says. "Earlier in the night, on that meadow over there, not indoors. Each time they say: this will be the last one. Yet they always come back, again and again, so it seems."

"Yes."

Silence.

They all look at one another.

"You came to destroy our unity."

"Yes."

"To introduce disorder and disharmony."

"Yes."

"Division, trouble in our unity?"

"Yes."

She pauses, their eyes always on her. Her returning gaze is vacant, empty.

"To divide and destroy?"

"Yes," says the Jew.

"And replace it with what?"

"With nothing."

All at once she moves as if disappearing, as if dying. Her voice quavers as she asks:

"Who has spoken?"

"Me," says the Jew.

She rises.

She looks at David.

·

"Jeanne is at the meeting," she says.

"With Gringo?"

"Yes."

"Gringo is at the meeting?" asks the Jew.

She does not answer right away. "I don't know."

"Jeanne is out in the streets, in the meetings, in the streets," says the Jew. "With Gringo."

"Yes."

She is not looking at anyone anymore. She looks out at the darkened street.

"Jeanne is out tonight," she says.

"Tonight there's the ice and the desolation," says Abahn.

"Jeanne is out in the ice and desolation," says the Jew.

Sabana's eyes grow wide.

"We're always afraid," says Sabana. "We never know what Jeanne does when night falls."

"You never know exactly where she is?"

"Never," says Sabana. She pauses. "She tries a little to prevent—" Sabana interrupts herself.

She is still looking out at the darkened road. "I'm afraid," she says. "With this old—"

"To prevent what?"

"Just a little, the death, here in Staadt."

Silence.

"He knows that?" asks Abahn, pointing to David.

"No."

"He doesn't know?" asks the Jew.

Sabana does not answer.

She turns toward the setting sun.

"She's young like David," she says. "Beautiful like David."

The setting sun reflects in Sabana's eyes, blue, dark.

"You live with them?"

"Yes," she says. "I'm there with them now. They have a spare room. They took me in. I make the meals. Jeanne arranged it with the government. I work in the morning. For the moment I am there with them. Jeanne and I, we are David's women, his wives."

They fall silent for a long moment.

"You said something?" asks Abahn.

"No," says Sabana.

"Then it was David?"

"No."

David has a tender expression on his face, at once attentive and joyful.

"When he isn't speaking, he's dreaming that he's speaking," says Abahn.

"He's in the process of speaking," says the Jew.

"It's true, if you go up close you can see it," says Sabana.

"He's listening, he's answering," says Abahn.

"Yes."

Sabana leans over David. The Jew watches her.

"What did you say, Sabana?"

"Nothing."

She rises. They look at her.

"What do you think?"

"Nothing."

They are silent once more. David cries out suddenly. He does not wake, just cries out a little.

•

Lingering scraps of daylight, glimmers of frost in the direction Sabana points, that of the dark field of the dead.

The darkness in the park is peaceful. The dogs of the Jew howl no more. Nor those in the field of the dead.

Abahn sits on the ground across from where David is. Leaning against the wall, he is silent.

The Jew stands, paces through the rooms.

Sabana sits at the table, follows him in the half-dark with her eyes.

"There was another man," says Sabana.

"He rests," says the Jew.

He walks with an even step. He passes in front of Sabana and then David, then he turns and comes back, pacing across the place. Disappearing and reappearing. She addresses him, her voice sleepy:

"You said you knew David?"

"To whom did I say that?"

"It doesn't matter to whom."

"I said I knew him a little." He walks past. She doesn't see him anymore.

"You said you knew me?"

"No. I saw you once one morning when you were cleaning at the Staadt town hall."

"You looked at me."

"I look at everyone."

He reappears. She is turned toward him. He does not pause.

"You didn't say: I knew her, not him."

"No."

She is silent. She does not see what he is looking at, paused at the doorway to the other room.

"And to us," she says, "to us they said, 'Forget the Jew, forget what he said about liberty, forget his name too.' You, you weren't able to forget a 'David'?"

"No."

She somehow becomes alert again. He asks:

"You have forgotten the Jew?"

"If they ask us to, they say, 'A Jew? Which one?' You wouldn't be able to say 'A David? Which one?'"

"I wouldn't say that."

He is still once more. They can barely see one another. She asks:

"Were you in Gringo's party before?"

"Yes."

"You were a Gringo."

"Yes."

"And you weren't able to say that you had never met a David?"

"No."

She rises. She crosses the room slowly, going toward the door to the park, pauses there. She says:

"David could be killed if anyone were to find out he was friends with a Jew." Her voice grows soft. "I want to understand this."

He moves toward her. She sees him coming. She waits for him.

"That's all false," he says. "David is in no danger of death because he knew a Jew."

He has come very close to her. She is looking at him still. She waits. Her eyes shine darkly in the reflection of frost on the grass.

"David is in danger of death because Gringo, on this night, needs someone to be in danger of death." His voice as soft and intense as hers. "There, in Staadt, David, who knew me, who knew the Jew: he took David."

They look at one another. They are silent. He asks:

"No one will ask me these questions, so why do I ask them of you?"

"Because it's night," says Sabana, and says nothing more.

She presses her forehead against the cold window, standing still.

"Leave me alone," she says.

She turns. He is still there. She lifts her hand to her face but does not touch it. He says:

"You said because it's night."

She does not answer. She takes a step. She is against the body of the Jew, resting there. Her hand, still raised, touches his frozen face. She says:

"I take yours, I take the words of a Jew-dog."

They are silent, entirely still.

"You want to live?"

He does not answer. And then:

"I want to live. I want to die."

Sabana's hand falls. She moves away. They are separate.

And the silence.

The dogs howl.

"You said because it's night."

"Yes. To dream of fear, we rise and wake up, we say that we dreamed, that it isn't true."

He walks away from her. He takes a step. She waits. He takes two steps. He walks. Instead of passing into the other room, he walks toward David. He turns on a lamp. He looks at David in the light.

Sabana moves. She takes a step, two steps, like him, she comes to look at David.

"Speak," she says, "He will wake up if we are too quiet."

The Jew speaks, slowly, always with the same soft tones. "He is in the Staadt Real Estate Society?"

"Yes, in that society. He is twenty-five. He's married to Jeanne. A laborer. He loves nothing but the forest and dogs."

She pauses, turns toward him.

"Speak. I will answer you."

They look at each other.

"You alone know?"

"Yes. He doesn't know."

"Supposedly he is honest, hardworking."

"Yes. They believe that of him. He believes it too."

A glimmer passes across the eyes of the Jew.

"You said the forest and dogs?"

"Dogs."

"He told me that at the café. He said, 'I know how to speak Portuguese and how to speak with dogs.'"

•

They are apart from each other. Again the Jew walks through the house.

Sabana sits at the table, away from him, away from David, next to Abahn. She waits. Listens: someone walking. Is it the steps of the Jew she hears? Yes, those. He passes before her.

"That one they sent to Prague," she says.

He stops. She gestures to David.

He walks again. Paces. She calls to him from where she sits, always with the same voice.

"You have been to all the capitals in the world?"

"Yes, all of them."

"The capital is everywhere."

"Yes."

A dull snapping sound comes from far off in the distance, from Staadt.

"The cold," she says.

"Yes."

He walks. He watches David. He asks, "He is in favor of the death of Jews?"

"He doesn't say anything about that," says Sabana.

He walks. She no longer follows with her eyes.

"You had a job once, a wife, some children? There, where you had been, you had the right to live and to die?"

"Yes."

"You fled? You left all that?"

"Yes. A long time ago."

"You said one day to someone in Staadt: 'I was hopeless, desperate.'"

"Yes."

"After you had again left the place you had been?"

"Yes."

"Always pursued? Killed?"

"Yes."

Silence.

"And for that they are killing you again?"

A painful smile drags across the face of the Jew.

"Yes."

"Desperation," repeats Sabana.

She falls silent. And then:

"And since you came to Staadt?"

"It's been bearable."

"Bearable even with the danger?"

"Yes."

He paces still. She watches him.

"Where you're always about to leave?"

"Wherever you are, I think, you are on your way."

Silence.

"I'm cold," says Sabana. "Afraid."

"We are afraid," says the Jew.

"Of death."

"Of life."

Silence. The Jew walks. Paces.

And then, while walking, right here, he calls out to David.

"David. David."

First quietly, and then louder and louder, he calls to David.

David sleeps. His lips are gently parted. His face captured in the lamp light turned on by the Jew.

"David."

He sleeps.

"David."

The Jews stops, waits. He sleeps still. The Jews begins pacing once more.

Sabana is silent.

"David. David."

Again he stops, the Jew. He stands still. Sabana struggles to discern him in the half-lit room. She hesitates, waiting. He paces away and then back. Sabana's eyes are two gray slashes devoid of light. He paces. He calls out. He stops again. They wait.

"David."

They wait. The cold grows in their hearts, in their wakes, a frozen climax. David's voice rises up in the silence.

"Yes, I hear you. What?"

His voice is quiet, peaceful.

The Jew has stopped. They hear a dull cry. It is not David. Another cry. The dogs howl out in response. The howling dies down. The silence freezes over, muffles it. The silence drags forth a sob from David's chest. Sabana's face contorts in pain. She says:

"It looks like he's suffering."

"Who?" asks the Jew.

She moves. She rises up and goes to the window. She passes by the Jew, she does not look at him, she is at the window, facing the empty street, lingering there.

•

The only sound is David's breathing, which occasionally stops as if bumping up against some barrier, and then begins again, longer, deeper.

"He's dreaming," says Sabana.

"Of what?"

"Cement. And dogs."

The Jew draws close to David. Sabana goes with him. They watch David.

"A thousand years?" the Jew says to David.

The hands of David flutter lightly.

"A thousand years," repeats David.

He sleeps.

His hands fall back to his body. The effort of articulating the words makes them tremble.

He is sleeping. He sleeps. His hands, his wounded hands, rest again on the arms of the chair. The eyes of the Jew are focused on the sleeping hands.

"A thousand thousand years?" the Jew continues.

It seems that David will speak.

No.

"A thousand thousand years?" continues the Jew.

A light tremor passes through David's body.

"A thousand thousand years," repeats David.

David's breath grows faster. Then stops. He does not take another.

The silence grows. It blinds. It sharpens to a peak. Spreads out. Spreads to the chink in the wall of slumber, a dull stone, a clamor, brief and strange.

David has cried out.

Having cried out, David thrashes in sleep, he lifts his head, his eyes open, he sees nothing, his head falls back, he speaks:

"Leave me alone," he begs.

In the silence that follows comes Sabana's rough voice:

"David."

And the voice of the Jew, the same:

"David."

Silence.

Abahn rises. He turns to face the dark road, his back turned to them. He says:

"And now falls the night."

•

The Jew walks away from Sabana and David. He

once more resumes his pacing through the house.

The wide stride of the Jew appears and disappears from the gaze of Sabana and Abahn.

Eyes closed, the Jew walks and talks to David.

"A thousand years? That's it? And it goes on?"

He speaks loudly. His voice echoes off the walls. Sabana stands looking out the window at the darkened park.

"A thousand years? A thousand years and it goes on?"

The peals of his voice resound from the walls.

"A thousand years more?"

Sabana looks away from the park, the dark ground, the earth, when the Jew cries out.

"David," cries the Jew. "David, David!"

He stops.

Abahn comes over as well.

"David," says Abahn.

Abahn does not cry out. Sabana returns. She sees that Abahn is talking to her. Sabana's blue gaze rests on Abahn.

Looking at Abahn, Sabana speaks to David. "David," she says, "The Jew is speaking to you?"

"Yes," says Abahn.

Sabana leaves the Jews and walks toward David. The Jews follow behind, allow her to approach alone. They linger behind her.

It is she who interrupts his reverie. She grabs hold of him, her hands on his shoulders. "Wake up, David. The Jew wants to talk to you."

David's head sags back and falls into sleep.

"David, the Jew wants to talk to you."

"No," says David, in his sleep.

Sabana releases his shoulders. She cradles his head. The hands of Sabana on David's head.

"The Jew is going to die, he wants to talk to you."

"No," says David, in his sleep.

She holds the head of David in her hands.

"He is going to die, he wants to talk to you."

She speaks in even tones.

David does not respond. He opens his eyes with a blank stare.

"You said a thousand years, why?" asks Sabana.

David answers:

"A thousand years."

She loosens her grip. She releases David's head.

She has released the head of David.

The head stays up. The eyes remain open.

Sabana turns, walks away.

Abahn and the Jew talk to David.

"You said cement, ice, wind, a thousand years?"

"A thousand years," David repeats.

"You said cement, fear, cement, fear, fear, cement, a thousand years? A thousand more years?"

David's eyes lift toward Abahn. Their color, David's eyes, is light blue, blue mixed with white.

Abahn draws close to David. The Jew is behind him.

Sabana stands over the Jew, next to him. Abahn and the Jew speak again to the sleeping David.

"You said a thousand years not hearing?"

"A thousand years not seeing?"

"A thousand years," David repeats.

"A thousand years the brain of an ape?"

David's blue eyes turn in the direction of the voice. He does not recognize it.

"A thousand years the ape Gringo?"

"A thousand years a killer? An ape killer?"

They do not say more. David's eyes are still open in the direction of the voice.

"David, you're David," It is the broken voice of the Jew.

"The hunter," says Abahn.

"The hunter," David repeats.

They fall silent. It must be this silence that then reveals an unease in David's fixed gaze. He has a stunned air about him, his stare questioning. He strains toward the voice. He sleeps, he says:

"The dogs."

Sabana takes a step toward the Jew. She does not take her eyes away from the darkened park.

It is Abahn who speaks to David. "You labor in the workshop of the merchants? You're twenty-five years old? Your wife is Jeanne?"

David responds in the same tone Abahn used, slowly and clearly:

"The dogs."

"You're a mason? You make cement? You work with the Portuguese? The Portuguese?"

"The dogs," says David.

He struggles against sleep. He articulates his words with difficulty. He finally makes a sentence.

"I want the dogs of the Jew."

He looks toward the rest of them with growing alarm. His gaze is clear and focused. One could say his stubbornness surprises him. He says again:

"I want the dogs."

He is quiet. He seems about to speak. He does not speak. He holds his head up. His eyes are open. He looks at Abahn with a questioning look.

The silence is unpierced. Then Abahn speaks.

"You've given the Jew to Gringo."

He answers without doubt in a simple, clear way. His response springs forth from sleep.

"Yes."

His eyes questioning still.

"The dogs."

He struggles visibly against immense fatigue. His eyes questioning still.

"Yes," says Abahn. "You gave up the Jew in order to have his dogs."

"Yes."

The softness of his voices is penetrating. Gratitude in his eyes.

"Listen," says Abahn. "David spoke. David said, 'I gave up the Jew in order to have his dogs.'"

"Yes," says David.

He is talking to Abahn without looking at him. Abahn looks deep into his eyes.

Sabana slumps against the body of the Jew. She continues to gaze out at the darkened park. The Jew is looking at David.

"David said, 'I repeated what the Jew said in the café,'" says Abahn. "'Gringo asked me and I repeated it. Gringo said that I had to make the connection and that it wasn't what the Jew said in the café, but a different thing. A simpler thing: that the Jew said one thing in the café but meant another.'"

Abahn pauses. David waits. He has a look of deep interest on his face. The pack roaming the field of death growl and bark out one after the other. The dogs in the park howl in response. Then, silence falls anew.

David calls out:

"Sabana!"

No one answers him.

"He said, 'I did what Gringo wanted,'" continues Abahn. "'I said the Jew offered me money if I would tell him what Gringo did with the other Jews. The Jew said to me: Freedom. Gringo said that what he meant was: money, money to leave Staadt if I gave up the names of the Jews who were executed.'"

David makes a great effort. He finds the words:

"No. The dogs."

"He said, 'I at once tried to say that the Jew proposed to give me the dogs if I gave up the names of the executed Jews, but Gringo said no: No, the Jew proposed to give you the dogs to sell for a high price. Don't forget, the Jew said he would give you money. Money.'"

"No, the dogs."

"Money," repeats Abahn.

David does not answer.

At any moment it seems sleep might finally overcome David. Abahn continues speaking in a low voice as if they were still in danger.

"He continued, 'Gringo asked Jeanne to make the connection. I didn't know. Gringo said that the Jew had gotten money from powerful foreigners. Jeanne had talked about this with Gringo. I didn't understand what Jeanne meant.'"

David's eyes fall from Abahn, search the shadows.

"Sabana!" he cries out in his sleep.

Sabana does not answer. He calls out again:

"Sabana!"

He falls silent. Abahn continues calmly:

"And he said, 'I didn't know what Gringo meant.'"

"Where is she?" David asks in his sleep.

Abahn does not answer him. He continues:

"David recounted, 'In the café the Jew said: I am hopeless, desperate.'"

"Sabana!" David cries out.

"He said, 'I didn't understand what the Jew meant,'" continues Abahn.

David does not cry out anymore. He has been conquered.

Slumber won, his head sags to the side.

"He said, 'Gringo told me: Forget this desperate, dirty word, this Jewish word.'"

Abahn tries to reach David faster than sleep.

"He said, 'I told all of this to Sabana.'"

"Sabana," murmurs David. "Sabana."

He struggles against sleep. His eyelids flutter.

"'And Sabana told me: Don't worry. David, you will have the dogs of the Jew. I will give them to you.'"

"Yes."

Sabana still looks out at the darkened park.

David leans his head against the back of the chair. His eyes are half-closed, his gaze toward Abahn, sleepy.

"He said, 'We speak of the Jews who will be executed. Gringo has forbidden it. We don't know why Gringo has forbidden it.'"

Abahn is quiet. He walks away from David. Does David see him leave?

"Sabana," David calls out again in his sleep.

David sees no more, his gaze floats away.

"Sabana!" His body turns toward her, he straightens up, his eyes becoming cloudy as if waking. He takes his gun, points it.

"Where is Sabana?"

He searches for her with his eyes.

His wakefulness is so brief, he looks too quickly to see her there, in the shadows, next to the Jew.

His hand releases the gun.

He falls in one quick movement back into the chair.

He sleeps.

•

Sabana leaves the Jew. She walks away from David to the table where the Jew sat.

The Jew stands where she left him, looking out toward the park.

Abahn walks once more between the rooms.

Sabana looks around. Abahn is out of sight, the Jew on the other side of the room. David sleeps. She is quiet for a long time. Then she speaks:

"He won't remember anything."

Her voice has changed, is low and brittle.

"He'll remember a little," says Abahn.

Sabana does not move. She too seems as if asleep. She moves no more than does David.

The Jew has turned. Abahn comes back. They look at her. She raises her eyes to them. Eyes like dark wounds.

"Give us the dogs," she says.

.

"Give your dogs to David," says Sabana. "Your dirty dogs, your Jew dogs."

The Jew comes toward Sabana. She watches him approach. She says to him:

"I'll wake him. I'll tell him you tried to run away. We'll take off with the dogs."

The Jew sits at Sabana's feet. He leans his head against her knees. He wraps his arms tightly around them.

"Your millions of dogs, you should give them to him. Write it down: I leave my dogs to David."

The Jew doesn't answer. His arms are locked around Sabana's body.

"You understand. Your dogs, your dirty dogs, your Jewish dogs, you should give them to him."

She does not try to wrench free from the grip of the Jew. She speaks without looking at him.

"The dogs are already David's. He gave them the Jew, so the dogs belong to him now."

Her voice is low and sleepy. She has the same blank stare as does David.

Abahn returns from the other room. She sees him. She speaks to him:

"I want the dogs of the Jew for David to go into the forest."

Abahn pauses in front of her and the Jew. He regards them both without responding.

"You brought these dogs with you and now they want to kill you. They want to get these dogs out of Staadt."

She pulls free from the Jew's embrace. She rises.

"You should give them to David before you die. If you give them to David they will live. You understand?"

She regards David.

"David will keep them safe from Gringo. He'll take them into the forest. They'll live."

She falls silent. Then starts speaking again:

"A kennel in the forest—he'll sell puppies, neither seen nor found out by anyone, secret dogs—he'll leave the mason work behind, goodbye to Gringo."

The Jew raises his head, he looks at her. He is listening with great attention. She begins to smile. There is a little spit on the corner of his lips. She addresses him:

"Maybe you don't understand? The dogs should be David's."

She waits. The Jew is still looking at her. He says:

"The dogs are David's. I'm giving them to him."

Sabana recoils. They look at one another.

"You will tell Gringo," says Abahn. "Write, 'The Jew has left his dogs to David.'"

The Jew rises, goes to the table and takes a blank sheet of paper, writes.

He finishes writing. He says:

"They will be happy."

She does not answer. Unmoving, she listens to them. She is regarding them.

"You have to explain to Gringo," says Abahn. "Tell him that David wanted the dogs of the Jew."

Slowly she turns back to the darkened park, stands there, gazing out. She says:

"Gringo won't listen. He won't read."

It seems they do not understand.

"You have to tell him that David's desire was stronger than life, stronger than death," says the Jew.

"It was a desire Gringo could not see," says Abahn, "but you saw it, Sabana. That David is a hunter. That he had the desire. That he should let David take the dogs."

"Because that name: David," says the Jew, "is the name of a hunter."

She says:

"These dogs are forbidden in Staadt. I found out."

They do not answer. They seem not to have heard. They seem to have forgotten Sabana. They talk among themselves.

"Dogs by the million," says the Jew.

Something breaks in the Jew's voice. What suddenly entered his voice?

"Jew dogs," says Abahn.

"Useless," says the Jew.

"Blameless," says Abahn.

"Happy," says the Jew.

Silence.

The sound of crying. They turn.

Sabana is crying.

Silence.

She says:

"I want the gas chamber. I want to die."

She cries out.

"Get me out of here. I want to leave."

They do not answer her.

·

"Which forest?" asks Abahn.

Tears fall from Sabina's eyes. She thinks on it.

"The forest."

"You don't know what's beyond here," says Abahn. "Where is the forest?"

She searches her thoughts.

"Where, I don't know. We have to talk about it."

"The wild forest," says the Jew.

"Yes," she says, pausing. "Where is it?"

"Deep within Staadt," says the Jew.

She isn't crying anymore. She looks at the Jews once more. Her gaze has become somber again, somber and blue.

"The forest is in David's mind as well," says the Jew.

She looks over at him slumbering.

"In David's head," she says.

They fall silent.

"You are in the forest," says the Jew. "You are in the head of David."

"Far away," says Abahn. "You see something."

She searches for a long time.

"I don't see another David," she says. "I see a Jew."

"There are Jews in the forest," says Abahn.

A sob, sudden, brief, stifled, all at once.

"They know it, just like David."

"You know it for David," says the Jew.

She is silent. For a long while she looks at the bare walls of the house of the Jew.

"The forest is in the house of the Jew," she says.

"Yes."

"In the body of the Jew, in his dogs," says Abahn.

Sabana's gaze unfocuses.

"In Prague, in the fields of the dead."

"Yes, like that. Prague is also Staadt," says Abahn.

"And the fields of the dead are in the house of the Jew."

"Yes."

"In an adjoining forest."

"In the forest," says the Jew.

.

They are all silent, separate from one another.

She is listening to the noise of Staadt. Everything is quiet.

She listens again, this time her eyes closed.

"You said something?" she asks the Jew.

"No."

"I heard. Someone speak."

He doesn't answer. She speaks to Abahn: "Someone said: treason. The treason of Jews."

"No," says the Jew. "No one said anything."

"Nobody spoke," says Abahn.

Suddenly a cacophony of barking from the dogs outside.

"In the barking of dogs I hear voices," says Sabana.

The dogs fall silent.

"They're quiet now," says the Jew.

"Listen," says Abahn. "No one is talking, there's no noise."

She listens: all is quiet.

"There was no betrayal by Jews," says Abahn. "There is the betrayal of Gringo. David gave up the Jew in order to have his dogs. But once he has the dogs, he'll give up Gringo. He'll say: Adieu cement, adieu Gringo."

Sabana turns toward Abahn, meets his eyes and smiles.

"At the risk of overanalyzing David, it's true that in the end you can count on saying adieu to Gringo," she says. "And then we will find the forest of the Jews?"

"Yes," says Abahn.

The dogs of the Jew growl, low and soft.

"It's Diane, she's dreaming," says the Jew.

Sabana once again remembers the park beyond. She points out at the invisible expanse beyond them in the dark, through the panes of glass in the door. She says:

"You said don't be afraid. But of what?"

"Of happiness," says the Jew.

"Of hunger," says Abahn.

David opens his eyes. The dogs are still growling. His eyes linger open.

"The word woke him up," says Abahn.

"Dogs," says Sabana.

"Hunger," says the Jew.

The dogs fall silent. They wait. The eyes of David flutter half-open, then suddenly close again. His breath evens out.

She gestures at him, says:

"And for this, you prefer hunger?"

"He prefers nothing, he prefers hunger."

"It's for that that they kill him."

"Yes."

Sabana gestures at David without looking at him. "For that, I prefer death."

"No," says the Jew.

They stand apart from one another. Each one alone. Each one looking at David, who is sleeping in the light.

"When they sleep," says Abahn.

Sabana looks away from David. She turns back to the darkened park.

"He is young still?" asks Abahn.

"Yes, young," says the Jew.

"When he isn't sleeping, he is a killer-ape," says Abahn.

"A stonemason," says the Jew. "A member of the Party."

"When he is sleeping, who is he?" asks Abahn.

Sabana is silent.

"The child of Sabana," says the Jew.

She is still there, in front of the door to the park, silent, staring out into the darkness.

•

Staadt is the entire darkened park.

The dogs of the Jew howl.

David's hand lifts gently as if pushing away the howls.

They are standing apart from David, their bodies separate.

"You went to start work," says Sabana. "You came back, you wrote. They saw you writing behind the windows of your house."

The dogs no longer howl. David has fallen again into sleep.

"I wasn't writing," says the Jew.

"In the night, at the table, everyone could see you. You wrote on blank paper."

She turns toward Abahn.

"Every night he walked back and forth in this house. He wrote. In the morning, he slept."

"I wrote what people said," says the Jew. "People said nothing."

Their voices are even, they sound the same.

"You wanted to write only what people said," says Sabana.

"No," says the Jew. "Not anymore."

"And what did people say?"

"Together or alone, they said the same thing."

"But even so upon returning here you wrote it down."

The Jew doesn't answer.

They are silent. From all sides, the constant dull pressure of the dark park. The Jew looks out at it through the windows. Sabana seems like she is waiting for something.

"Yes," says the Jew. "I wrote it."

They are silent once more.

"Gringo said he comes a little before sunrise?" asks the Jew.

"I don't know," says Sabana.

Silence. There is some subtle change in their voices.

"Did you think they would say something?" Abahn asks.

"I thought nothing like that," says the Jew.

"Before coming to Staadt?" asks Sabana.

"I was told there was no point in trying. But I never tried to write what people said."

The Jew points at something on the table.

"The papers are right there," he says. "They won't have to look for them."

"They will burn them," says Sabana.

"Yes."

"When they burn them," says Abahn, "Gringo will say, 'The Jew has written a secret journal. In this journal he has said how he contacted foreign powers.'"

"Yes," said the Jew.

"Every time they each speak of the figures in the journal," says Sabana.

Silence.

"And they won't understand," says Sabana.

"They won't," agrees the Jew.

A tight smile stretches across the face of the Jew.

"They will burn your things as well," says Sabana. "Your furniture, your clothes. They won't leave anything whole. They'll destroy the dogs."

"David's dogs," says Abahn. "David's forest."

"Yes."

Silence. Then Sabana rises, goes toward the door to the park.

"It wasn't interesting, what people were saying in Staadt?"

"It still isn't," says the Jew.

"So that's interesting to whom?" asks Sabana.

"Everyone," says the Jew.

"To burn it, then?"

"Sure," says the Jew, "to look at it, as well."

"And for the ones who said it all, the people of Staadt?"

"No," says the Jew.

"It's not interesting for anyone," says Sabana.

She moans a single word. A brief sob, mournful, low: "David."

Deep in slumber, David moans at the same time, long, seemingly without end: an unknown dream without a doubt. No one notices the dream.

They are silent.

"There has to be time," says the Jew.

He points toward David.

"So David can . . . David, David . . ."

He does not finish his sentence.

•

It is Abahn who takes up the charred papers lying on the table. He reads:

"We reached the eighth floor on January 18ᵗʰ. The walls were not yet built. The wind blew through. Winter was hard. We drank alcohol at all hours. In the evenings, we were drunk. The Portuguese are not used to it, this cold. Three Portuguese at the site died. Five of the Africans froze to death in their room. The Greeks aren't used to it either. There was one of them in my room and he coughed all the time. My site is number three. At seven in the morning it was less than 12 degrees. We do less work than we could in the summer, the cold cracks the skin of your hands, the cement you poured into the cracks, gray, the morning, cracked skin. Gringo is the head of site number three. Jeanne taught the Portuguese how to write. Gringo said that site number three creates honor for the Party. He sent a list of our names to the city. We petitioned the city. Gringo wrote out the petitions. He said, 'The conditions of the Portuguese are unacceptable.' Gringo spoke to the House of the People. He spoke all night to the 22nd Congress of the House of the People. We were exhausted that evening. So sleepy. At the end of all this, we carried cement, thirty times ten kilos of it. That's three hundred kilos. Our hands burned from it. From the moment you can't manage anymore you're just like the Portuguese."

In the silence David cries out. "The dogs!" he calls out in his sleep.

The dogs howl in the dark expanse. A single howl.

"Gringo," says Sabana.

She doesn't move, she doesn't take her eyes off the Jew.

The dogs fall silent.

David falls back into his fitful sleep.

"They bark at night whenever someone passes by," says Abahn.

"No," says Sabana, "they mark the passage of Gringo."

She listens intently in the direction of the pathway outside. The Jews are not paying attention.

"He's looking at you," she says.

She is listening with her eyes closed.

"He's alone."

She listens again in the direction of the road. The Jews are not paying attention.

"He was alone. He's gone now."

Silence anew.

"Maybe it was someone else," says Abahn. "Or it was nothing."

"In Staadt," Sabana says, "we recognize every sound. Even Gringo walking past. He came to see."

.

"**I**s that all there was to read?" asks Abahn.

The Jew takes some time to respond. "There were some other things about the working conditions."

They are silent, the three of them, standing apart from one another, unmoving.

"The dogs aren't barking anymore," says Sabana.

"We could read," says the Jew.

"Someone could talk," says Abahn.

"Or cry," says Sabana, "for the dogs."

"They are on the table, under the scorched pages," says the Jew.

They are, all three of them, caught in the same languor.

"The Realtors Society," begins Abahn.

He stops. Begins again:

"The Realtors Society was created for three industries. It grew from strong investments. A pharmaceutical company, French. A

German company, cellulose. And an American company, tungsten."

He pauses. Silence.

"Go on," says the Jew.

"Yes, go on."

Abahn goes on, with a growing languor:

"The payout, at this level of investment is a strong 52 percent. The legal percentage of payout has been fixed at 27 percent, the legal fees comprise the 25 percent remaining."

He pauses. Sabana says:

"I knew about the pharmaceutical company."

"Keep going," says the Jew.

"The Realtors Society," continues Abahn, "was built on top of the old cemetery in Staadt. Permits to build were given in four days. The commissioners and three municipal councilmembers were able to raise three and a half million. At this level that sum has tripled."

He pauses.

"And," says the Jew.

"The Portuguese," Abahn continues, "the Portuguese and others paid the syndicate's tariffs. They were not given the right to vote. They had no right to strike. The foreigners are 70 percent of the workforce, so the company is immune to strike."

He stops. Closes his eyes.

The Jew says nothing more.

"The most recent contract provides for 12 percent overtime pay past 40 hours, but it has not been honored."

Pauses.

"The value of untaxed products has already increased 10 percent. For the non-foreign worker the increase is already resolved."

He pauses.

Abahn pauses and then begins again. His voice is weak:

"So the single major policy issue is the sliding scale of the minimum wage."

He stops.

•

Abahn still sits at the table as if he were reading from the charred papers.

The Jew takes some steps and then sits against the door to the darkened park. He stays there, on the ground, his head turned toward Sabana, his eyes closed.

Sabana makes the same effort. She rises. She walks with purpose. She turns toward the Jew. She listens. She stands there, near to him, she studies him. She says:

"Turn on the lights. I can't see you."

He does not move. Neither does Abahn.

Sabana turns and switches on the light next to the Jews.

She looks from one to the other in the shadowy light that falls across their faces and closed eyes. Then she sees only the Jew. Says:

"I'm looking. I see you."

Abahn.

"He isn't thinking anymore."

The Jew's eyes are closed. She says:

"No. That's not right."

The Jew opens his eyes.

"You're afraid," cries Sabana. "Where were you?"

"Here, in front of you," Abahn says.

"Not him," she gestures at the other. "Not him."

The Jew and Sabana regard each other. A tight smile spreads across the Jew's face.

"One day I'm going to kill myself," says the Jew.

Sabana's intense gaze flares blue and then fades.

"It's for that reason exactly that they want to kill you."

"Yes," says Abahn.

Sabana sits next to the Jew. She stays there, next to him, quiet, her eyes open.

They are silent. Both fallen against the walls, looking at nothing.

"The Jews still cannot escape madness and sorrow," says Abahn.

He pauses. He speaks with concerted effort:

"Sometimes it's so difficult for them to live."

Silence.

"Before, the Jew was so sure," says Abahn.

"Of what?"

"He was with Gringo's Party."

"Communist."

"No. With Gringo."

She struggles to speak clearly the same way Abahn had:

"And now? He's what?"

Abahn does not respond right away.

"If he's anything, he's a communist," she says.

Abahn rises, rests his back against the wall that opens to the park. He feels apart from the others. Sabana hears him from across that distance.

"And now?" she repeats.

The Jew smiles, makes a little gesture.

"*Nothing more?*" she demands.

"No," says Abahn. "*Something else.* But he doesn't know what."

"I knew it," says Sabana.

Abahn slides down the wall and lands once more on the floor. He is still a little apart from Sabana and the Jew but like them he is on the ground, fallen.

Sabana's hand lifts and brushes across the eyes of the Jew.

"You've gone blind."

"Yes," says Abahn.

"You've become deaf."

"Yes."

The hand rests on the closed eyes.

"Like David," says Sabana.

The hand falls back.

•

She does it. With great difficulty, she gets up and moves away from the Jew.

She stands facing him.

She turns from him toward David, but her eyes stay fixed on the Jew.

Then she turns toward David, pauses there, turned toward him. Finally, her eyes unlatch from the gaze of the Jew.

All falls still.

Sabana's body seems to tremble between turning to David and turning back to the Jew.

Then, suddenly, she chooses. She moves slowly toward David. Pauses. Moves. Comes close to David, studying him.

His breath is long and even. He sleeps a deep sleep. She watches him.

She does it.

Slowly, she cradles David's head in her hands and lifts it.

"Wake up, David. The Jews are talking."

"No," David mutters in his sleep.

She leans closer and forces a light tone into her voice. "David, the Jews are talking."

"What?" David asks.

His eyes are still closed.

"What?" he asks.

He opens his eyes. He looks over at the Jews sitting on the floor. He seems to recognize them. And remember them. They do not return his gaze.

For a moment it seems David is resting.

"They are not trying to escape?" he asks.

"No."

She fixes her attention on him. "You slept well."

David doesn't answer.

"What time is it?" he asks.

"Night," Sabana says.

David glances repeatedly toward the darkened park where the dogs are.

"And Gringo?"

"He passed by," she says. "He'll come back later."

"Their meeting is still going on?"

David is stunned.

"Why so long?"

"I don't know," Sabana says.

"He told me at the beginning of the night," says David.

He looks over at the Jews.

"This whole time there's only been one Jew," he says.

"Gringo sent the second while you were asleep."

David gets up. He stretches his arms, grimaces, looks at his hands, flexes them. He doesn't feel well. Suddenly he freezes. He has thought of something.

"The second Jew. Are they going to kill him too?"

"I don't know."

"Whether they kill him," David smiles, "or only the first one, it's all the same to them."

"Yes," says Sabana.

The Jews have raised their eyes. They do not look at David, they look toward the darkened park. They are silent.

"Do they know each other?" asks David.

"I don't think so."

Abahn smiles at Sabana. David sees the smile.

"Look, they're smiling," says David.

She does not respond.

"Why are they smiling?" he asks.

She does not answer.

"At the moment of death," he adds.

David seems uncertain. He is about to smile as well, but does not. It is as if he is intimidated. He ought to see that she has not responded. He says:

"You woke me up, you told me, 'the Jew is talking.'"

He points at the Jew and says:

"He's laughing."

The Jew's eyes are closed. His face is expressionless.

"He was talking," says Sabana. "He was talking about killing himself. That's why he was laughing."

David is still frozen in place. He points at the Jew and says again:

"He's laughing."

"A person might laugh if he's some hours from death," says Sabana.

They look at the Jew. His eyes are fixed on the darkened park and it seems he might be laughing.

"He was laughing," David says. "I see him laughing."

David, still frozen, is completely fixated on the Jew.

"Maybe he's really asleep," David mumbles.

"No," says Sabana.

"Maybe he's afraid," says David.

"He didn't try to run away," Abahn points out.

David starts in surprise. His eyes shift to the new person, Abahn, and then back to the Jew.

Sabana says, "He said, 'I want to live, I want to die.'"

"Maybe he doesn't care which," David says.

"Maybe."

Sabana leaves David. She walks toward the back of the room and sits down against a wall. David finds himself alone in the light.

Silence.

No one speaks.

David waits. There is an obvious awkwardness.

"I don't understand," David says. "You told me the Jew was speaking to me."

"You can't force him to say more," says Sabana.

David addresses Abahn. "What did he say?"

"He said, 'Nothing. Something else. Otherwise. Somewhere else.'"

David looks from one Jew the other, and then at Sabana. He wants to laugh. He says:

"You woke me up for this?"

No one answers him. He sees the Jew looking at him. He starts. The Jew is not looking at him anymore. The Jew closes his eyes. For the first time it seems a great effort for David to speak.

"Who is he?" David asks.

"I don't know him," says Abahn.

"I don't know," says Sabana.

"His life is invisible," says Abahn.

Silence.

"Who are you?" Sabana asks the Jew.

The Jew shakes his head.

"He has no more courage," says David.

"Yes," says Abahn. "His strength is still there. Still present."

David studies the Jew who is smiling, his eyes closed, and realizes the strength within him.

"It's true," says David.

"It's just momentary. It will pass," says Sabana.

"The dead of the night," says Abahn.

The Jew rises, takes a few steps, slowly, distracted it seems, his shadow falling over David, he turns toward the door to the darkened park. Pauses there.

"He wants to live," says Sabana. "And he won't make the effort to do so."

Silence.

David leans forward out of the light.

"He wants to live in the *banlieues* of Staadt without working," Abahn says slowly. "To live without work at all, without any occupation, to live like that in the *banlieues* of Staadt."

"Without any work at all," murmurs David.

David looks again at the Jew. He wants to say something. He says nothing. He stares with a tangible intensity at the back of the Jew.

"One night," says Sabana, "I wasn't here, where was I? Just hanging about? You were going to the café, you and the Jew, he was telling you a little bit about his situation."

David's face grows pale.

"I didn't listen," says David. "I didn't understand."

"None of it?" Sabana asks.

"He must have heard some of it," comments Abahn.

David thinks for a while.

"Something about freedom," says David at last. "Something about liberty."

He thinks again.

"About despair," says David. He seems confused, intimidated. He smiles. "Then I slept."

They are silent. Abahn gestures toward the Jew.

"He's unsure now. That's what I think."

David thinks.

"It's completely normal for Gringo to kill him."

"Normal," says Abahn.

David lowers his voice a little:

"He's Gringo's enemy."

"He's a different kind of man," says Abahn. "He's a communist who believes that communism is impossible. And Gringo thinks it is."

David smiles as if at a joke. He hesitates.

"Yes, definitely," he says.

"Which?" Abahn asks.

David stops smiling. He looks toward Sabana. He wants her help. She is silent.

"You don't know," says Abahn. "We don't know."

They are silent. Again Abahn gestures toward the Jew:

"He doesn't think it's worth the trouble to kill Gringo."

"He thinks Gringo is dead," says Sabana.

"What? How?" cries David.

No one answers him.

"It's completely normal that Gringo would kill him," says David again, his voice trembling.

"Yes. Gringo," says Sabana.

David stares at Sabana in terror, seized by brutal shock.

He waits. Sabana says no more. His terror grows.

"The life of the Jew is unseeable, invisible." says Abahn. "Like the life of David."

His terror grows still. Silence falls.

"Before, the Jew was so sure. Like Gringo is now," says Sabana.

"Of what?"

"Of what we would find after the wait. And of where only the wait could lead."

"And when the Jew was very young," asks Sabana, "did he believe as Gringo does now?"

"Yes," says Abahn. "He came to this conclusion after a number of years."

"I don't understand," says David.

"For a long time. Gringo. A long time, you understand."

David does not answer.

"We believed in the wait, logical and unending. Now we believe it's useless," says Abahn.

David thinks on this. He searches the faces around him. "What happened?" he wants to know.

"Patience became our goal."

David shakes his head brusquely, grabs his gun, releases it as if were aflame: it's the Jew who has spoken. His voice is soft.

"I found this patience," says Sabana.

David's glare shifts abruptly to Sabana.

"Patience burned your hand," she adds.

Silence.

"It's possible we were wrong," says Abahn.

"Yes," agrees the Jew. "Possible. Always possible."

.

The Jew returns slowly to his place. He sits on the ground, leans back against the wall. A tight smile spreads across his face. He says:

"It's been a while."

He closes his eyes.

Sabana turns to the window that looks out onto the road. She hears the baying dogs out on the field of the dead.

"David I see outside," she says. "I see that if we open up then the cold comes in. You, you see David in David."

"Yes," says the Jew.

"David, you're David," murmurs David.

He looks at them, an unanswered question hovering. He tries to figure out what he said.

"He saw that you were young," says Abahn. "He saw you as a child. He wanted to know your name. He's crying. He has seen evil."

"He cried," murmured David.

"Yes. Now he sees you better."

Silence, all at once and deep. The dogs bark no more. No one breathes.

"How does he see me?" mutters David.

The Jew opens his eyes and looks at David. David and the Jew look at each other for the first time.

"I want to kill you," says the Jew.

His voice cracks. Love, once again, comes into the voice of the Jew.

David stretches out an arm and calls out:

"Sabana!"

She does not answer.

"You were sleeping," says Abahn. "He saw your sleeping body only. He saw your hands."

Silence. Far off in the distance the dogs howl madly.

"And now suddenly we are uncertain about the fate of David," says Abahn.

David sits up in his chair, looks over at Sabana and opens his mouth as if to cry out. He does not.

Silence then.

The voice of Sabana:

"I'm afraid."

"We are afraid," says the Jew.

Sabana takes a few steps, stops by the window, turns her face toward the cold glass.

"No one but Gringo can live outside."

"And Jeanne."

"Yes."

She listens. Her voice dwindles.

"The wild animals break free in the forest." She listens. "The pools and ponds overflow."

"It's a profound slumber," says Abahn, "at the end of the night."

Their voices seem identical, slow, even. David cries out:

"Come!"

She does not hear him. He searches her face. She has turned away. She looks at the Jew.

The Jew is looking back at her.

"The Jew used to believe that success was real," says Abahn. "Not anymore."

David does not respond, does not acknowledge them at all.

"He thinks now that success is a failure," says Abahn. "That the greater, more obvious success is the greater and more serious failure."

"Strength," says the Jew.

David, one more time, touches his gun.

"Death," says the Jew.

David yanks his hand back as if the gun were a flame.

"I saw," says Sabana. "I saw it."

"Quiet," David begs her.

"It burned your hand," Sabana says.

.

No one speaks.

The dogs howl.

"Gringo may turn back in the cold," says Sabana.

She leaves the window, returns to her place on the floor, leaning back against the wall.

"Sabana!" David calls out.

"I don't hear you anymore," she says.

"Come over."

"She won't come anymore," says Abahn.

David doesn't ask again.

"The love she had for David has, this night, turned into love for the Jew," says Abahn.

"Shut up, you," mutters David.

And then the voice of the Jew, breaking, muted:

"Sabana."

And then the voice of Sabana:

"I will be killed along with the Jew."

Silence.

"Who said that?" asks David.

"Sabana," says Abahn.

"She's crazy," says David.

Again the voice of Sabana:

"Gringo will shoot from the road in front."

David, quiet for a moment, suddenly bursts out:

"She's crazy when she's like this."

No one replies. He goes on.

"She doesn't understand anything."

"Sabana," says the Jew.

"She doesn't know how to read," says David, "she doesn't know anything." He addresses Sabana, "Do you know where Staadt is?"

"I don't."

David laughs, a short, fake laugh, and then stops sharply.

"Look," he says. He is talking to the Jews. He speaks so quickly. "She doesn't know how old she is, she doesn't even know her name."

He stops. Then speaks again, a little slower.

"She doesn't know if she has a child."

Sabana does not reply. David speaks directly to the Jews.

"She doesn't know where she came from, look at her."

He waits. Sabana has been quiet.

"Some say she's Jewish," says David. "That she came from far away."

"From the German Jewry," says the Jew. "From the town of Auschstaadt."

David pauses. Then repeats slowly:

"Auschstaadt."

His frenzy has dissipated.

He turns to Sabana. Fear rises in her eyes. He asks her:

"Are you from Auschstaadt?"

They all look at her. She is frozen, sitting there against the wall, in the light. The clear blue eyes are unfocused: they seek Auschstaadt.

"Auschstaadt," she repeats.

"Yes," says the Jew.

"Where is Auschstaadt?" asks David.

"Here," says the Jew.

"Everywhere," says Abahn. "Like Gringo. Like the Jew. Like David."

"Here. Everywhere," says the Jew.

Sabana is still thinking about Auschstaadt.

"And when?" asks David.

"Always," says the Jew. "Right now."

"We're all from Auschstaadt," says Abahn.

Silence. A new fear seems to grow in David.

"She wouldn't be any different from the Jew if she knew something," says Abahn.

David recoils, still looking at the form of Sabana on the ground, leaning back, as if he recognizes something evil in her. He says:

"It's true, Gringo said she was crazy, that she makes things up."

"What do you think?" asks Abahn.

David makes an effort to speak. The fear retreats a little. He tries to pull his thoughts together. He answers without looking up:

"I don't know." He smiles a tight and painful smile. "I amuse myself with her."

Silence.

"Who is she?" demands David.

The fear has gone.

"No one knows," says the Jew.

David and the Jew look up at one another.

•

David and the Jew are looking at each other
still.

"You have to try anyway," says the Jew to David.

David starts to attention.

"What?"

"To move toward communism," says the Jew.

"To *where?*" David smiles as if it were a joke. The Jews smile
too.

"To where we don't know," says Abahn. "You don't know."

The Jew smiles, at David, at everyone.

"You have to try not to create it," says the Jew.

Unthinking, David strokes his gun. Having found it again,
he yanks his hand back as if burned.

"To arrive in the forest," says Abahn.

"Wild," says the Jew.

"The forest," David repeats.

They fall silent. David is still looking at them. They look
elsewhere.

"You came to destroy our unity," says David. His voice is dull,
flat. Trembling.

"Yes."

"To divide? Sow dissent in our unity?"

"Yes," says the Jew.

"To sow dissent in our spirit?"

"Yes."

"To what end?" asks David.

"No one knows," says the Jew.

"To break, to shatter," says Sabana.

"Where?" asks David.

"To Sabana," says the Jew.

Silence. David fights against sleep.

"It would be normal to kill you, to hunt you like a pest."

"Yes," says the Jew.

Silence.

Sabana looks through the dark window.

David stands up.

Sabana and David can hear what the Jews do not hear, see what the Jews do not see.

"We walk by the ponds," says Sabana.

"There's a light!" David calls out.

She turns back to the window, the darkened park, the field of the dead.

"There's a light out in the field," says David.

Sabana peers out, listening. "I saw it," she says calmly. "It's not there anymore."

He turns to her. She is still there, at the window, looking out at the field.

"I'm afraid," says David. "Come over here."

"No."

He collapses back into his chair. He closes his eyes. With all his strength he tries to fall asleep again. He calls out to Sabana. He tells her to come back to him, he says he doesn't understand.

She does not answer.

He calls again, weaker. Then he calls to her no more.

She turns toward him, sleep is overcoming him, his arms again on the armrests, his face fallen. She leaves the window, goes to his side, she takes his hand, sits next to him.

"Don't fall asleep," says Sabana.

"No," says David.

•

Sabana stays with David.

"Don't fall asleep," she says.

"No," says David.

She holds his hand in her own. She says:

"The light in the field wasn't real. Your hands are so cold."

He does not answer.

"You're less afraid," she says.

He turns an inquiring look upon her.

"I think so," he says.

The Jews are at the table, in the same position. Heads resting back against the wall, they are silent. The Jew looks at Sabana, her blue eyes, dark, blue, fixed upon David.

"You must not be afraid," she says to David.

"No."

There is a look of complete confidence on David's face. She takes his hand, she studies it.

"Your hands are so heavy," she says. "It's the cement."

"It set," he says.

"You work so much," she says.

"Yes."

"Why?"

He pauses before answering:

"I don't know."

Silence.

Sabana holds David's hand in hers and looks toward the road. She speaks, her voice even and low:

"Tonight, in the frost and ice, in the desolate cold, there is Jeanne, out in the cold desolation."

"Jeanne?" asks David. "Where?"

He almost cries it out. His voice sounds dull, broken.

"I'm not sure," says Sabana. "You forgot," she says to the Jew, "we're afraid for Jeanne, night and day."

"Why?" asks David.

Sabana doesn't answer David. She speaks to the Jew. "She works against Gringo, she's trying to subvert him, she's trying day after day."

David pulls his hand from Sabana.

"That's not true!" he cries.

Sabana does not answer. Her gaze is fixed, her voice broken, like David's.

"She thinks she can. She's crazy."

Silence.

"When Jeanne gave her report tonight, I wasn't sleeping," says Sabana. She gestures at David. "David was sleeping. But I heard. Gringo told her to write down 'criminal lies,' but she wrote 'criminal liberties.' Gringo wanted her to say 'in service of the great power of the merchants,' but she wrote 'the ideological aberration.' Gringo cried out. Jeanne said she went to wake up David to ask him what the Jew said in the café, and after she wrote exactly what David said. Gringo laughed. He told Jeanne not to treat him like a child. Then Jeanne wrote the word, 'liberty.'"

Sabana leaves David's side and walks over to the door that opens onto the darkened park.

"Jeanne doesn't know that I know," she says, turning toward David. "You didn't know."

"No," says David. He waits. The intensity of his waiting slowly shows in his face.

"You don't know anything?" she asks.

"A little. I came to know," he admits. "Gringo did say once that Jeanne was useless, a wreck."

Silence.

"Jeanne is young, like David," says Sabana. "She is the same age as him. Beautiful like him." She looks at the Jew. "And one day they will kill her like they will kill you."

"Shut up!" cries David.

Sabana turns to the darkened park.

"We live together," she says. "We are both David's wives."

A sob bursts from her chest. She presses her palms against the cold glass of the window. Then presses them to her forehead.

A racket bursts out in the part of Staadt beyond the darkened park.

"There's shooting!" cries David. "Near the ponds!"

Sabana does not move. David's face has again taken on the expression of a child.

"What are you afraid of?" asks the Jew.

David does not answer. He stares at the Jew. His gaze wavers.

Sabana returns to David's side.

.

Again the cry of a dog. In the field. A strange cry, a strangled bark, a whine.

"Diane," says David.

"You were still sleeping?" Sabana asks.

David sits up with difficulty.

"I heard you from far off," he says to her, "as if you were on the other side of the park."

"With the dogs."

He listens.

"Diane. It's Diane." He starts as if seeing Sabana for the first time by his side. "Oh, there you are."

"She is dreaming, the dogs are dreaming," Sabana says.

"No," says David.

"Or Gringo is trying to kill her."

David starts and then suddenly calms.

"No. No."

"They didn't say anything about killing the dogs," says Sabana.

"No," says David.

Sabana turns from David. She goes to the door opening out onto the park. She looks out into the darkness. The cries cease.

"This dog of the Jew's, Diane," she murmurs, "has love in her voice."

"Yes," says David. "A kind of smile in her eyes."

"A dog for you to play with," she says.

"Yes."

"But they'll kill her," Sabana says. "They want only guard dogs here. There are a hundred of them in the field of the dead. The princes of Staadt."

David listens to the soft, quiet voice of Sabana. Her hands quivering.

"They eat everyday," she says. "They sleep. They train at sunrise. Sometimes, they put them in the police tanks going to the Jewish neighborhoods. Gringo showers them with praise, throws flowers on them, gives them medals, hangs them on their collars."

She takes a few steps toward David, then stops before reaching him. They look at one another. She says:

"Sometimes they are free, they release them, they say: 'You are free, go kill.' When the Jews pass through the barbed wire on the other side of the field, where the ponds are, we say to them: Go kill."

"'You are free,'" repeats the Jew.

David rises. His eyes are flat, opaque. He searches for his gun. Sabana doesn't seem to have noticed him moving. She says:

"You are free."

David releases his gun. He looks at Sabana, standing before him. His hands tremble. He smiles at Sabana, a tight and empty smile:

"I don't understand," he says.

"You didn't shoot," she says.

Silence.

In the park, that same sad howl.

"Diane," says the Jew.

David turns to look at the Jew, then at Sabana. His gaze focuses and sharpens.

"She cries from despair," says Sabana.

"A dog?" David asks.

"One can never know" says the Jew.

"A dog crying from despair?" David murmurs to himself.

"Who can ever know," says Abahn.

.

Silence.

"What time is it?" asks David.

The voice of Abahn:

"Nearly day."

David sits up straight, frightened. He looks toward the road for the first time. He trembles.

"No, it's still night," says the Jew.

"There's no more shooting near the ponds," says Sabana. "They've left again."

"I don't understand," David murmurs.

They are silent.

This time, in the park, a long plaintive cry. David straightens, says to the Jew:

"They're hurting Diane."

The Jew, like him, is listening to the cry. David turns toward Abahn.

"Is she crying out because of the night? The cold?" asks Abahn.

"I don't know," says the Jew.

"From fear, I think," says David.

"That she'll be killed?"

"That there will be killing," says Sabana slowly. She falls silent. She has gone back to sleep.

·

The silence.

Sabana leaves David, moving slowly toward the table, to the area where the Jews are. She turns back to him. She seems worried, bothered. "The Jew is going to give you his dogs. You can have them."

David's air changes. Happiness seems to break out over him, in his eyes, mixed with the sadness.

"Diane," says Sabana. "You could take her."

David waves his hand to silence her.

"Diane," she repeats, "the Jew's dog. She could be yours."

The softness of her voice brings tears to his eyes.

"What are you doing in the house of the Jew?" she asks, "Leave though the forest."

He shakes his head: no. He says, "Gringo would never want that."

Silence.

"You know the forest?" asks Abahn.

"Yes," says David. "Beyond the barbed wire."

"Big?" Sabana asks.

"Wild," says David.

"There are jackrabbits."

"Yes."

They are silent before this unchanging dream, desperate. Their eyes fixed on some indefinite point in the darkness outside.

"Who told you this?" asks Abahn.

"No one."

He looks out at the dark park.

"*It's impossible*," he says.

"Dogs, gassed," says Sabana softly. "Millions of them."

"Yes," says David.

They look at the Jew. His eyes are closed.

"They have been in the family for a thousand years," says Abahn. "They are part of it. Gringo will set a price."

"How?" asks David in a child's voice.

"From the moment he kills them, he ought to explain why," continues Abahn. "He will say: I kill them because they are worth so much."

"Such a rich sum," says Sabana.

Silence. The Jew has opened his eyes and is looking at David.

"I't's starting up again," says Sabana.

Sabana can hear things that David can't.

She listens. "The bullets ricochet off the ice. They are on the other side of the park." She listens again. David watches her. "They're gone," she says.

"Again," David murmurs.

"Yes."

"I don't understand," David says to the Jew.

Sabana goes to him, she stops just before reaching him. "You ought to do it," she says in a low voice.

Almost imperceptibly, he recoils, never taking his eyes off her. "What?" he asks.

"Kill the dogs of the Jew."

David doesn't move. Fear leaves him.

"You could say to Gringo: I killed the dogs of the Jew as well."

David is still staring at Sabana. The fear builds. Like a smile. He sees the blue of her eyes fade out.

"Gringo would promote you in rank, you could leave off the work with cement, rejoin the Red Army."

David lifts his calloused hands, he pushes the image away, he cries out.

"NO," he bellows, his hands raised, his eyes closed against the vision of a dog, killed, executed.

Then he falls silent, his hands fall and grip the armrests of the chair.

He looks over at the Jews.

.

"He is crying," says Sabana.

The eyes of the Jew are closed.

"There's crying," says Sabana. "Someone is crying. It's either you or him."

She turns toward David. David doesn't understand. He passes his hand over his face, he looks at the wet hand. He doesn't understand.

Abahn, sitting next to the Jew, seems to have forgotten him.

"Or he's sleeping," says Sabana.

She pauses, looks at the Jew.

"No. He's crying. About you. Or about nothing." Her tone grows soft. "About nothing."

David leans toward the Jew. His face has a pained expression. "He's not trying to protect himself."

"No."

Sabana and David watch the Jew. Abahn speaks without looking at him.

"He is afraid," David murmurs.

"He didn't try to escape," says Abahn. "He has no reason to feel fear."

"He's exhausted."

"No. Look at him. He's still strong, still vibrant."

David examines the Jew with the closed eyes, discovers the strength there.

"It's true," he murmurs.

"The life he's led ought to have prepared him for what awaits him," says Abahn.

They are silent.

"But who is he?" David asks again.

"I don't know," says Abahn.

"He was bored of the Jewry," says Sabana, "of life wandering on the road. That's why he came here."

She turns to Abahn. She says:

"That's you as well, the Jew."

"Yes," says Abahn. "Me too."

All these words sink into David: he looks at the Jew, just him. Still staring at him, he says:

"Gringo said, 'the Jew is dangerous.'"

"Yes," says Abahn.

"Still?" asks David.

"Yes."

David keeps looking, looking, and somehow strangely he sees, sees the danger.

"It's true," David murmurs.

With difficulty he turns to Abahn and says:

"Gringo is afraid of him."

"Gringo doesn't exist to the Jew."

David remembers.

"It's true, the Jew never said anything at all about Gringo, nothing bad ever."

Abahn smiles, is slow to respond.

"The only way Gringo exists for the Jew is that he is going to kill him."

Fear seizes David once more. It is almost as if he is going to jump up from the chair. Neither Sabana nor Abahn notice his movements.

"Otherwise," says Abahn, "the life of the Jew is as invisible as the life of David."

"A mountain of pain," says Sabana.

"A mountain of cement," says Abahn.

"Mountains of the cement of pain," says Sabana.

"Yes," says Abahn, smiling, "Invisible, drowned in the Jews."

The Jew lifts his head and looks over at David.

David notices the Jew looking at him. With a sudden start he tries to evade his gaze. He falls back into the chair. The Jew swings his gaze toward the door out to the darkened park. David calms.

•

"He didn't know where to go," says Abahn, "so he came here, to Staadt. He could have gone anywhere, but it would have been the same: other Gringos and merchant's unions and they would have wanted to kill him too. Here, there, it's all the same."

Again David tries to rise up out of the chair. Again he fails. Again neither Sabana nor Abahn notice him.

The Jew has once again rested his head on his arms. He seems exhausted. Sabana sits at the table, leaning against him. She strokes his back, his hair, his hands, his body. Then she lets her hand drop, rests there without moving.

David sees only the Jew.

"It's been a long time since he left home," Abahn says. "He had a wife once, children. Then one day he left."

"Then he left the place he had gone to," adds Sabana.

"Again and again," says Abahn. "Left from every place."

An anxiety builds in David's eyes.

"And once, a long time ago, he'd had a profession. He's begun, these days, to forget even what it was. He said once to someone in the village: I forget now what I once did before."

Silence.

"He said that to you, David?" asks Sabana.

With difficulty, the word comes from David:

"Yes."

"He also said that he studied. For a long time. In many capital cities. He said: It pleased me to study. No he's forgotten what all he studied. He said to someone in the village: I can't remember anymore what I once knew."

"He said that to me," says David.

The dogs howl.

The dogs howl: David turns his gaze toward the door to the darkened park.

The howling subsides.

"He said: I began to think about where I learned this word— 'Jew.'"

A shot rings out near the ponds, disrupting the Staadt night. Shots heard again from even farther off. No one hears the shot near the ponds.

"There's something written on his body," says Sabana, "on his arms, there's something written."

She sits up and takes his arm, folds back the sleeve of his jacket and looks at his forearm.

"It's written where the number would be."

"Written where you arrive," says Abahn, "in the capital of the world."

Sabana looks at the arm.

"It's written in blue."

"What?" asks David.

"I don't understand it," she says. "I can't read it."

"It's the word: NO," says Abahn.

"When did they write it?" asks David.

"At some point during his life," says Abahn.

"It's the same word for the Jew and for those who want to kill him," says Sabana.

"The same," says Abahn. "The word of the Jew and the word of those against the Jew."

Sabana replaces the arm of the Jew and sits back, closing her eyes again, resting.

Abahn and Sabana both seem to be in the same exhausted state.

"He had these stories," says Abahn, "a hundred of them but all the same, those of the Jews. He has barely told any of them to the people of Staadt. He told them instead about the lives of others."

David nods.

"Before coming here the Jew was released from all parties, Gringo's and others, and all his stories were finished, he was left with only his own. The Jew couldn't stand, one more time, to be alone with his own story. So he started again. He began to become a man of Staadt."

Abahn pauses. He speaks with a great tiredness sweeping through him, slower. He looks down at the ground. He no longer seems to be speaking to David alone.

"With forgetfulness descending everywhere, this new thing became possible—to become a man of Staadt. So he did it. Began once more to become a man of another new place."

Abahn pauses.

"He wanted to live," says Sabana.

"Yes," says Abahn. "He wanted to live without working in the *banlieues* of Staadt. To exist without working at all, without any occupation but that of living, in the *banlieues* of Staadt. And he decided to do it like this from now on."

Silence.

"Just like that? Why?" asks David.

"It was his unchangeable desire. His purest desire."

Silence.

"That's terrible," murmurs David. "To do nothing."

"No," says Abahn, looking at David. "He spoke."

David struggles, searches in the emptiness.

"He said to us: Leave it all behind."

David speaks but he doesn't know what he says. He trembles.

"He said: Look here, leave it all, you're building on ruins."

In the half-light someone laughs. It's the Jew.

Joy floods David's face. He cries out, "He hears us, he laughs!"

One after the other they all start laughing with the Jew.

"He said: Enough with this foolishness. Leave the cement behind."

"Leave the cement behind," says the Jew.

"He said: Go hunt."

"Go hunt," says the Jew.

"It's he who spoke to me in the forest," cries David. "About the jackrabbits. He said, keep going, they're beyond the barbed wire."

"Beyond it," says the Jew.

"He spoke of the light in the forest," says David, remembering, speaking slower now, "of summer also."

"Summer," says the Jew.

Silence.

The broken voice of the Jew then rises:

"David's summer."

Someone is shooting near the ponds.

They speak no more. David listens and trembles. Sabana, sitting next to the Jew, also listens. Her voice then rises:

"What is Gringo waiting for?"

The shots cease.

•

Abahn is speaking to David, still overcome by exhaustion. "First he forgets what work he did. Then he forgets about money. Then he forgets what he learned. Finally, at the end, he forgets his wife, his children. He said, 'I couldn't lie in front of them the way I could when I was away from them.' Is that what he told you, David?"

"Yes."

"And he left so his children would also leave, later on."

"Then he left again and again," says Sabana.

"Yes," Abahn says. "Again."

"He lingered among the Jews, burned Jews and gassed Jews, with or without God."

"Yes," says Abahn. "He was searching."

"It's Staadt where he will die," says Sabana, "in the penal colony on the road to the Jewish capital."

Silence. Abahn does not continue. David waits.

The silence hovers between them. Abahn closes his eyes. He seems exhausted. David realizes he is lonely, alone, broken down.

Then Abahn continues:

"I know nothing of life."

Silence. No motion at all on David's smooth and pale face.

"I don't know anything about my life any more," says Abahn. "I will die without knowing."

David says:

"It doesn't matter."

"Nothing," says Abahn. "In the end: nothing."

"Me either," says David. "I don't know anything either."

"No, you don't."

"No."

•

Abahn speaks to the Jew in a slow and even voice. "It's because you came here that we understand a little more. We know some names, some dates."

"Yes," says David.

"You came here one night. You walked the village all that night and all the morning that followed. People met you. They remembered. You smiled." He pauses. "It was the morning of the second day that Gringo recognized you."

He pauses.

"Yes," says David.

"Gringo said, 'No talking to the traitor, no going to see him, no looking at him. He was in the Party and he betrayed it.'" Abahn looks at the Jew. "Did you know that Gringo recognized you?"

Abahn answers for the Jew, saying to David:

"He knew. He knew that whenever he went out that he would be recognized."

Far off, on the field of the dead, the dogs cry out, howling.

"You bought this house, a bed, a table, chairs. You stayed here for many days. You burned things, the papers—only after you had started preparations to leave. But it was already too late. Gringo had already alerted the workers of Staadt to your presence."

He pauses. Says:

"In your life, you kept only guard dogs." Turning to David, he says, "Why?"

"He played with them in the evening."

"The dogs didn't know," Abahn says.

"No."

"They didn't know that he is Jewish. Neither did you, David?"

"No," says David.

Silence.

"Many days passed," says Abahn. "Many weeks. Many months. The autumn."

Silence once more. David waits, sitting up in his chair, his eyes tense.

"Afterward, a long time after, Gringo said to you, 'You're talking to the traitor? You're listening to what the Jew says? You don't know what he did?' You said you didn't know. Gringo was amazed. He said, 'How? Everyone knows. He questions the Party line on the Soviet concentration camps. You don't know this?'"

Abahn's voice cracks in places. He gasps for air. He breathes with difficulty.

"You didn't understand what Gringo said to you. That the Jew was what he still is: any Jew."

"Yes."

Abahn gasps for air. There is nearly no air.

"You spoke with him again. Against Gringo's orders, you kept speaking with the Jew because the Jew had dogs."

"No!" cries David.

"And that was forbidden also."

David nods weakly.

Abahn wants to speak more. He struggles to get there, he gets it out quickly because once more he can, he gives it to David in clear phrases.

"You didn't covet the Jew's dogs. You just wanted to speak to someone who had dogs."

David nods.

"Afterward, a while after, Gringo spoke of making the Jew disappear, you thought then for a moment, you might have his dogs."

David nods yes.

Abahn stops talking to David and starts talking about him instead.

"Right after Gringo's order David went to the café with the Jew, just like before. It was that very night in the café that the Jew spoke to him about freedom. He said, 'Your wounded hands are your own hands, David.'"

David nods. Abahn gulps air and continues, talking faster.

"The Jew said, 'In their suffering and their joy, in their madness and their love, in their freedom these hands are your hands, no other's, the hands of David.'" He pauses. "It's because he said these things that the Jew will be killed."

A sob heaves in David's chest.

It's a brief, isolated sob, broken, quick.

Abahn speaks again, more hurried:

"You didn't understand what the Jew meant."

David does not react.

"You repeated it without knowing what it was you were repeating. You told Gringo. Gringo said, 'YOU LACK AN EDUCATION IN POLITICS. WE WILL KILL THE JEW AND THEN YOU WILL UNDERSTAND.' It was Jeanne who reported this."

David folds over himself violently, his arms wrapping under his legs. He trembles then as if he were going to break. His face contorts like a drowning man's.

"I haven't taught you anything," says Abahn. "*You knew everything.*"

David doesn't answer him, doesn't hear him.

Abahn falls silent.

David cries out something like, "I never had a dog."

He heard his own cry.

He lingers, rising toward this cry, in the position of someone crying out still. He rises, searching the air for this cry, searching and finding tears.

David doesn't know he is crying. His tears fall.

Within the tears one hears the names of Sabana and the Jew.

Sabana rises. She stands behind the windows looking out toward the darkened park, the field of the dead. She looks at nothing else.

The Jew lifts his head. He heard the voice of Sabana:

"I will be killed along with the Jew."

The Jew looks past her toward the darkened park.

The shooting out near the ponds has broken out again.

·

The shooting stops.

David's tears flow more slowly, coursing.

David seems preyed upon by a terrible dream. His head thrashes, shakes no. His hands seek out things no one else but he can see. His face seems to be speaking, answering something.

Then his tears trickle off. Then the movements of his face and eyes calm as well. The dream drifts off.

He seems to see no more. He releases his legs, turns his face back to the light, rests back against the chair, limp, completely spent.

The silence. They are all silent. The Jew looks at David. Sabana and Abahn seem not to notice.

The shooting begins again.

The deafening sound of bullets cracking out from their shells. David listens to them in seeming distress. He moves no more than Sabana or the Jews.

Diane howls to death.

The cracking of bullets continues at irregular intervals. Some shots closer in the park. No one in the house of Abahn seems to pay any attention to the shooting in the park.

"He arrives."

Abahn and Sabana both turn to the one who has spoken: David.

The shooting gets closer, Diane still howling to death. A funereal moan cuts across the night of Staadt.

And then:

"If someone is killed, then run off through the other door."

The voice of the Jew.

"Release the dogs, go by the ponds."

Again, the Jew.

David turns his head. He has heard.

Slowly, he gathers his strength, he tries to pull himself up out of the chair. He falls back. He does not move.

The shooting gets closer and closer to the house of Abahn.

David, once more, makes an attempt. He grabs hold of the armrests with his hands, swollen by the work with cement, and lifts up his body.

He stands.

He finds himself upright once more in the room. He does not move. He looks at the Jew. His hands are hanging, swollen. He listens to Gringo's shots over the ice of the pond. He alone knows what those shots mean.

"He's the only one armed. It's the same gun firing."

Another shot, the dogs howling.

"Go," says the Jew, "do whatever you have to." He pauses. "By any means, try to live."

"Yes," David says to the Jew.

David closes his eyes, tries to separate Gringo's shots from the howling of the dogs, he tries to calculate the distance, plan out the course.

"He is shooting in the direction of the field." He opens his eyes, looks at the Jew. "Talk to me."

"If you succeed and live," says the Jew, "tell this story."

"Yes."

"Tell it. To everyone. Without distrust. Look around you. Closely. All this is destroyed."

"Yes."

Silence. Diane is no longer howling. There's no shooting anymore, either. David listens.

"He is still coming. We have five minutes."

David hasn't taken his eyes off the Jew; all the while he has been listening to the turmoil of the Staadt night.

"He shoots because he is afraid," says David.

"Yes."

"He should be alone," says David. "There's no group. He made it up to make us believe he was busy. For me to be left alone with you, with a gun and the Jew."

"Yes."

The dogs, once more, howl.

"Leave your work," says the Jew. "It's difficult to do, but try."

"Yes."

"And your fear. And your hunger."

"Yes."

Silence. Gringo approaches without firing.

"Don't be alone," says the Jew. "That's what I'm telling you. Leave that behind too."

David does not answer.

"I don't speak to you in your position but to myself if I were David. Not otherwise. You, do what you like. Go back to Gringo if that's your plan."

Silence.

Suddenly a shot rings out quite close to the house.

"I told you this in the forest," says the Jew.

"Yes," says David. "It feels far."

"Far off, through the place of Jews."

A shot hits the outside wall of the house.

Sabana and the Jew seem neither to have heard nor understood.

"He's walking in front of the windows," says David. "Flatten yourself against the wall."

The Jew does not move. Neither does Sabana.

"I can't see anything anymore," cries out David. "I can't see the Jew."

Someone walks on the road a few meters in front of the house.

David says:

"He's here."

•

And now, the first cry through the howling of the dogs.

"David!"

"There is the brother, the ape," says Abahn.

Sabana turns to look toward the road.

Abahn and David turn that way, too.

The Jew stops looking at David, he turns toward the darkened park.

They stay like that, as they are, scattered throughout the room, unmoving. Sabana next to the Jew, behind the bare windows. They all have the same expression of rapt attention.

The fear grows no more.

"David!"

The voice is getting closer. Still, that long howling of dogs in the park. The shooting has stopped.

"Three minutes," says David.

"It's daybreak," says Sabana.

Beyond the road, toward the barbed wire, flush with the sky, with the growing light, still dark.

They talk, first one, then the others.

"He isn't shooting through the windows."

"He isn't shooting."

The howls of the dogs die down.

"He's out there. He's watching us. He isn't shooting."

"This is the lost time," says Abahn. "The dead time."

Some steps on the road.

"He's leaving."

More steps.

"He's coming back."

"What's he looking for? The house of the Jew?"

The steps approach once more but this time more sure. The steps come all the way to the door.

"He hasn't fired the gun," David says.

He listens. Says:

"He's afraid."

"Of you," says Abahn. "Of David."

Someone calls out.

"David!"

David takes a step toward the door. He stops. He says slowly, sharply, "I HAVE NOT KILLED THE JEW."

Silence on the other side of the door. There is no response to what David said. David starts up again:

"YOU SAW THROUGH THE WINDOW THAT THE JEW STILL LIVES."

Silence on the other side of the door. No one responds to what David said.

There is a cry:

"There's no point in hiding! We saw you!"

David doesn't understand.

Silence.

David takes another step toward the door.

Silence still.

Then the voice of the Jew, slow, calming:

"We will walk past the ponds, we will walk north."

David turns roughly toward the Jew: his eyes are closed, he's not looking anywhere.

"Open up! It's useless to hide! Open up!"

David advances again. He says:

"The door's open."

Silence. No one opens the door. No one responds to David.

"We will escape the field of death," the Jew continues, "the dogs on the field of death." His voice suddenly empties of its calm. "We will try."

David turns once more. The Jew has the same expression still. Sabana's gaze shifts from the door to the Jew.

Once more from behind the door comes a cry, very loud:

"It's useless to deny it! You have been seen! Open up!"

Silence.

Silence behind the door. David's fear returns. He takes his gun in his hand and calls out:

"The door is open! Come in!"

Silence.

Again the voice of the Jew:

"We will try not to build it. We will try."

David holsters his gun. He turns back to the Jew. A wild spark of savage joy flashes across his eyes.

Sabana understands then that there is another person behind the door.

"Jeanne is with him," she says.

Suddenly, on the other side of the door, Gringo's voice bursts out; to David it is as if he has never heard it before:

"We demand that the Jew return David!"

David listens to the voice with great attention.

"David must return!"

David isn't listening to the voice anymore.

"Dirty Jew, you better give David back!"

"We will try," says the Jew, his voice breaking.

David isn't listening to the voice anymore. He looks at the Jew.

"Yes," says David.

"David has to come back!"

"We will find the forest," says the Jew.

"Yes," cries David.

"Dirty Jew! You give back David!"

The Jew lifts his eyes, looks toward the road, the dawning day, the invisible border, he does not hear Gringo. A painful smile—as exhausted and light as his voice—draws across his face. Sabana watches him.

"You dirty traitor! Give back David!"

"We will live," says the Jew. In the silence between the cries his voice is just a murmur. "We will try."

"Yes!" cries David.

David is overtaken by an involuntary shudder. His face grimaces in silence and then: David laughs.

"David is ours! David must be returned!"

At first timid, still mired in tears, the laughing slowly bursts forth from David's body, from the cement and stone. The dogs cry out. Laughter issues from David in hiccups. The dogs start to howl in accompaniment with the violin sounds of Gringo's shouts.

"David!"

David's laughter takes its shape. No longer smothered. David's entire body shakes with laughter.

In the half-light another laughter is heard: Abahn. The laughter of David and Abahn goes through the doors of the house of the Jew.

"David, come back!"

The laughter of Abahn and David passes through the walls, unrolls in the half-night of Staadt, spreads across the field of death.

"David!"

The laughter stills the howling.

"David."

The voice is colorless, just like that: the anger fading, the voice is Gringo's again.

"I want to speak in the name of our great Party. I will do my duty."

The laughter comes again, irrepressible, crazy, child-like, mixing with the howling of the dogs, breaking apart the conversation, order, sense, meaning, light. It is the laughter of pure joy.

"Before we took over   bad element   bad worker   he stole from the warehouses of Staadt   unworthy worker   without class consciousness   without valid professional training   with individual morality   without a future   from the Technical School of Staadt   out of all the sites in the region   whim   criminal dilettantism   the arrival of the Jew   of the traitor   for the first time in his life   kept his job   David was well taken care of   two years yes two years   spirit of anarchy and insubordination that increased David's misfortune   Two years yes of efforts all right   the result was worth the trouble."

Silence.

The howling of the dogs dies down. The howling of a man this time:

"Dirty Jew! Dog! I'll teach you that a revolutionary doesn't give up to anyone! Another six months and David will have you shot, you and your dogs!"

The howling stops.

Silence.

"Open it," says David.

Silence.

David laughs again.

"I'm going to open the door," says David, still laughing.

He smiles still.

"I'm opening it!" cries David.

Silence. They wait.

"He's gone," says David.

They wait longer. Steps resound on the cobblestones, rapid. They turn, see a shadow pass, etched onto the half-light of the new day.

Abahn and David walk to the table in the shadowy light, they fall into the chair there, laughter of joy still covering their faces.

The Jew goes to the door.

Sabana follows him.

"Jeanne," says the Jew.

They are standing in front of the door, where David just was.

No response.

"Are you there?"

"Yes," says Jeanne. And after a moment: "He's gone."

She falls silent.

"It's you?" the Jew asks again.

"Yes."

"It's you," says Sabana.

The voice of Jeanne is heavy, slow, already seized by the ice of death.

"Don't open the door," she says. "I'm not coming in."

The Jew listens to the voice of Jeanne. He does not answer.

"He went a little far," Jeanne said. "He spoke in anger because you were laughing."

"You lie," the Jew says lightly.

Jeanne does not answer.

"I want to hear your voice," the Jew says. "You're David's wife."

"Yes. Sabana and I."

Silence.

"Forget what he said," says Jeanne.

"He didn't listen. He didn't hear," says Sabana.

"The way I want to understand your voice," says the Jew.

Jeanne pauses a moment, then says, "I don't want to meet you."

"He knows," says Sabana.

They wait for Jeanne to speak.

"Gringo is gone to the House of the People. Their meeting is still going on. I should go there and join him."

Silence.

"He has to report on David's mission," says Jeanne. "I should go there." She pauses. "I'm going to go."

"There's no meeting," says the Jew.

Silence.

"Are you still there?" asks Sabana. "I can hear you."

"Yes."

Silence.

"What are you waiting for?" asks the Jew. "You can speak without fear."

"For Sabana to speak to me," says Jeanne.

Sabana hesitates.

"David isn't coming back," she says finally.

A sob is heard. Sabana and the Jew go closer to the door.

"Never?" asks Jeanne.

"Never," says Sabana. "He doesn't fully realize it yet. I'll explain it to him later."

They do not hear anything from Jeanne. They are still there, against the door.

"I'll stay with him," says Sabana.

A brief moan.

"Whatever happens," says Sabana, "from now on I'll stay with the Jews."

Silence.

"Why?" asks Jeanne.

"They love everyone," says Sabana.

Silence.

Jeanne says, "They want the world to end."

"Yes," says Sabana.

Silence.

"You want to say something more?" Sabana asks.

"Pay attention," says Jeanne.

"Yes," says the Jew.

"What else?" Sabana asks.

"The dogs."

"David moved the kennels behind the garages yesterday," says Sabana, "in the night."

"That's better," says Jeanne.

She falls silent.

"What else?"

"Return to your life," says Jeanne. "Don't leave Staadt before nightfall. I won't leave until your departure." She pauses. "And above all . . ."

"Yes?"

"STAY TOGETHER," says Jeanne. "DON'T LEAVE ONE ANOTHER."

"Yes," says the Jew.

She falls silent. The Jew calls out:

"You cannot help but follow him?"

There is a long silence. Then: "No. I am Gringo as well. The female Gringo."

She pauses and then:

"But I'm barren. I can't bear children."

She pauses again but speaks no more. They do not press her with any more questions.

She stands there still, silent, just like them.

Then in the silence they hear her body move. She is walking away from the door.

Then, light footsteps on the cobblestone, hers.

Sabana turns back to the field of the dead.

The Jew slowly straightens up. He does not try to make out through the window the form passing by. He does not move. He seems indifferent to everything around him. He has left once more, left again, now he is with her, the one walking away on the deserted road in the new day dawning on Staadt, once more anew in his life.

Acknowledgments

An excerpt appeared in *Clockhouse*.

Douglas A. Martin gave me encouragement and feedback at the right moment. Jeffrey Zuckerman read an earlier draft and gave invaluable feedback, corrections and suggestions. I am indebted to his keen eye. At every thorny moment when I could not bridge the gap between Duras's extremely subtle poetic mind and her clean and spare prose style, Nathanaël was there, sometimes to salve, sometimes to scold, but always to guide me toward a deeper and more difficult relationship to the text.

I also thank Libby Murphy, who was my co-translator on *L'Amour*. Working with her on that project made me feel capable to tackle this one on my own. Certainly throughout this work I felt her influence and sensibility as a translator guiding me.

There is a sideways debt I offer to Ananda Devi, whose powerful book of poetry and prose *When the Night Agrees to Speak to Me* I was translating simultaneously. Her sensibility drew me through languages to find this book in English.

Finally, I want to thank Open Letter Books and Chad and Kaija, who are so devoted to literature in translation and to Duras in particular.

M arguerite Duras was born in Giadinh, Vietnam (then Indochina) to French parents. During her lifetime she wrote dozens of plays, film scripts, and novels, including *The Ravishing of Lol Stein*, *The Sea Wall*, and *Hiroshima, Mon Amour*, and was associated with the nouveau roman (or new novel) French literary movement. Duras is probably most well known for *The Lover*, an autobiographical work that received the Goncourt prize in 1984 and was made into a film in 1992. She died in Paris in 1996 at the age of 81.

Kazim Ali is a poet, essayist, and novelist. In addition to his own writing, he has published a translation of *Water's Footfall* by Sohrab Sepehri, and, along with Libby Murphy, he translated *L'Amour* by Margeurite Duras, which is also available from Open Letter.

OPEN
LETTER

WWW.OPENLETTERBOOKS.ORG

**OPEN
LETTER**

WWW.OPENLETTERBOOKS.ORG